A HOUSE WITH A PAST PUTS FEAR INTO THE PRESENT

The first thing Kathy noticed was the cold.

It was a strange sort of cold. Sudden. Enveloping. Silent. Secret.

Timothy, standing in the hall just a few feet away, was saying something, but his voice seemed distant and distorted.

Around her, the silence deepened and grew more intense, so intense that Kathy could actually hear it, a faint hissing whine, like a television that's just been turned on and is warming up.

That's when she felt . . . no, *knew* . . . that someone was listening. That she had tapped into another dimension. Another place. A place where someone or something was listening.

"Kathy!" Timothy's voice broke through the cold, listening silence that surrounded her. "Kathy!"

Don't miss these terrifying thrillers by
Edgar Award Nominee
Bebe Faas Rice

Class Trip
Class Trip II
Love You to Death
The Listeners

Available from HarperPaperbacks

THE LISTENERS

Bebe Faas Rice

HarperPaperbacks
A Division of HarperCollinsPublishers

This is a work of fiction. The characters, incidents, and dialogues are products of the author's imagination and are not to be construed as real. Any resemblance to actual events or persons, living or dead, is entirely coincidental.

HarperPaperbacks *A Division of* HarperCollins*Publishers*
10 East 53rd Street, New York, N.Y. 10022

Cover illustration by Jeff Walker

First printing: March 1996

Printed in the United States of America

HarperPaperbacks and colophon are trademarks of HarperCollins*Publishers*

❖ 10 9 8 7 6 5 4 3 2 1

To my father, Laughlin John Faas
with love and gratitude

"Is there anybody there?" said the Traveler,
Knocking on the moonlit door . . .

. . . But only a host of phantom listeners
That dwelt in the lone house then
Stood listening in the quiet of the moonlight
To that voice from the world of men . . .

—*The Listeners* by Walter de la Mare

1

The man pauses in the open doorway of his home. His pale, thin hand trembles on the doorknob.

Have I left anything undone? he asks himself. No, I have followed Their instructions carefully. They will be pleased with me.

Then he frowns and cocks his head, listening.

"Is anybody there?" he calls through the half-opened door.

In the hall, in the heavy silence, the grandfather clock clears its throat and chimes the hour.

"Is anybody there?" the man calls again.

No reply.

He shakes his head, confused.

"My family is ... gone," he murmurs. "So why do I feel they are all there, upstairs, on the landing ... listening?"

He hesitates a moment longer. No. There's no one here. There can't be. Not now.

He closes the door behind him, locks it carefully and walks to his car. He guns the motor and, without a backward glance, drives off.

Within the house, the listening silence continues . . .

2

NOVEMBER, 1995

"We're almost there," Kathy Colby's father announced. "Only a few more blocks."

Mrs. Colby turned around in the front seat and smiled at Kathy and seven-year-old Timothy. "You're going to love the new house, kids," she said.

Kathy smothered a sigh. Her mother had been saying that all the way from North Carolina, where they used to live—to Brentwood, Virginia, their future home.

"Beth says that whenever *they* move, she can spot their new house a mile off. It's always the worst looking one on the block," Kathy said.

Mrs. Colby laughed. "Well, that won't be the case with us. And I think Beth is probably exaggerating a little, don't you?"

Just talking about Beth made Kathy's heart contract in a spasm of loneliness, as if someone had placed a cold hand on it and squeezed hard.

That was the hardest part of this move. Leaving good friends behind. Friends like Beth. Especially Beth. She'd never had a close friend quite like her before. She'd miss Beth more than anyone.

Beth's father was in the army and they moved frequently. Beth, in an attempt to cheer Kathy, had said, "It's not as bad as it seems, Kathy. I've gone to a lot of schools, and you *do* make new friends. I didn't want to move here, but then I met you, and I wouldn't have missed that for anything. You're going to make lots of new friends, too, and get involved in all sorts of fun things."

"But I don't want any new friends," Kathy had protested tearfully. "I just want to stay here with my old ones. My junior year's going to be awful without you and the rest of the gang. I hate the idea of being the new girl in some ratty school, especially since I'll be coming in after school's already started."

"That won't matter. It's only early November. And believe me, Brentwood is *not* ratty," Beth said, rolling her eyes expressively. "It's one of those posh little Virginia hunt-country suburbs close to Washington, D.C., where everyone's either a congressman, a diplomat or a foreign service officer. One of my mother's friends used to live there and she absolutely *adored* it."

Posh? Beth must be mistaken about Brentwood. Kathy's family could never afford to live in a place like that. Maybe Beth's mother's friend had stretched the truth in an attempt to impress them.

But I hope Beth's right about the new friends and the fun stuff at my new school, Kathy thought. Even if she isn't, there's no point sulking and making Mom and Dad miserable.

As she'd told Beth, "We don't have any choice about the move, anyway. When Dad's company filed for bankruptcy, he and at least a hundred others lost their jobs. He and Mom were really worried there for a while. But thanks to Uncle Ned, Dad was able to find something else. And on a higher level this time, too. It pays a lot more than the old one."

The only catch was that it was in Washington, D.C. The Colbys would have to relocate.

Kathy's mother and father had flown up to Washington three weeks ago and found a house that Mrs. Colby claimed was "too good to be true."

"It's perfect," she'd said. "It's in a small, lovely town on the Virginia side of D.C. That whole area is one big suburb of Washington, you know. Your father says he won't mind the commute."

Finding a house they could afford had been the biggest problem facing the Colby family. Kathy couldn't believe that her parents had solved it so easily. Especially when Beth told her how expensive Brentwood was.

Mrs. Colby kept saying how beautiful the house was, too. How could that be? In order to sell the old one quickly, they'd had to drop the price way below market price. There wasn't much left over, once they'd paid off the old loan, to put down on a new house. How great a house could they get on such a small down payment? And in Brentwood?

Something was wrong. Definitely wrong. But what?

Maybe Mom wasn't exaggerating. Maybe the house really *was* everything she said it was. And maybe this meant things were starting to look up for them. Maybe the house was a sign. An omen.

And maybe she'd be happy here, after all.

Maybe.

The sigh she'd been trying to hold back these many miles finally slipped out.

Beside her, Timothy leaned forward and stared out at the street.

"Is it that one, Mommy?" he asked anxiously, pointing to a large ranch-style house. "Is that one ours?"

"Not yet, Timmy," Mrs. Colby said over her shoulder. "We're not there yet."

Her voice was cheerful. Teasing.

It struck Kathy that maybe her mother was acting just a little *too* cheerful. Why? To make them think that they were all going to love it here in Brentwood?

Poor little Timothy, Kathy thought. Leaving my old friends and starting a new school will be hard enough for me, but it's going to be even harder for him, poor little scrap.

Scrap. Poor little scrap. That's what she'd heard a neighbor call Timothy once, not realizing Kathy was listening.

"What a poor little scrap that Timothy is," Mrs. Kelly had said. "He acts like he's scared of his own shadow, and he walks around in a world of his own. I've even seen him talking to himself . . . "

Kathy had never liked Mrs. Kelly after that. Yes, she'd thought, Timmy *was* overly sensitive and imaginative, but he'd grow out of it in time. After all, he was still little. Not even six years old yet and—she had to admit this—pretty immature for his age at that.

But Timothy did *not* talk to himself. Not really. Mrs. Kelly must have seen him talking to one of his imaginary friends. He did that sometimes. He'd make up these imaginary friends and believe in them so strongly that he could even tell you what they looked like.

This had worried Kathy's parents at first. They'd discussed it with a child psychologist. He'd told them that some children—lonely, overly imaginative ones—often created their own playmates to take the place of the real friends they lacked.

"He'll settle in with his school friends one of these days and forget all about those dream children he's created," the doctor said. "In the meantime, however, you should see that he has opportunities to be around lots of other children. Talk to his teacher. Make her aware of Timothy's special problem. He's a very intelligent little boy. Very creative. This is just a phase . . . "

But Timothy was seven now, and still shy.

Still immature for his age. Still relying on his imaginary playmates.

How much longer? Kathy's parents kept asking themselves. Timmy ought to be blossoming out a little by now, hadn't he? Making friends. Running with a pack of noisy little boys.

What are we doing wrong?

And now the move. Heaven only knew what that would do to him, but what else could they do?

I won't let myself worry about that right now, Kathy told herself with a mental shrug, feeling a little like Scarlett O'Hara. Well, Scarlett was sixteen, too, just like her, when she met Rhett Butler and all her adventures began. Not that she expected to find someone like *him* hanging around the junior class at Brentwood High.

"This is it," her father called out. "The new homestead."

He made a left turn into the driveway and stopped, so that everyone could get a clear view of the house.

Mom was right. It *was* gorgeous. And it was big—bigger than Kathy had expected, and it stood on a wide, well-landscaped lot. A Colonial, Mrs. Colby had called it: two-storied, brick, painted white, with intriguing little gables and pointed eaves, shutters on all the windows and a red front door.

Red. The color of blood . . .

Kathy shivered. Now why on earth did she think that? Actually, the red door was more a

Colonial Williamsburg color. Muted. Not at all like blood.

Mrs. Colby opened the door on her side of the car and deposited Mitzi, the family dog, on the ground.

"Okay, Mitzi. Run. Do your thing. See that nice big bush over there? It's all yours now, sweetie."

Mitzi, a small black cockapoo, was growing old and arthritic and had spent the trip spaced out on baby aspirin, her head resting on Mrs. Colby's lap.

She looked around, puzzled, at her new surroundings and then attempted to crawl back into the car.

"I guess she doesn't know it's home yet," Mrs. Colby said. Then, proudly, "Well? What do you think of the house, kids?"

"It . . . it's wonderful!" Kathy said breathlessly, staring at the house, taking it all in. Its size. The large yard. The lovely neighborhood.

Prestigious. Yes, that's what you'd call it. *Prestigious.* She'd seen pictures of homes described like that in the real estate section of the newspaper back home.

No, not back home. That wasn't home anymore. This was home. She and poor little Mitzi would have to get used to that fact now.

Funny about that door thing, though. Why did it make her think of . . . ?

"I like it," Timothy said, almost whispering, his eyes wide. He pointed to one of the dormer windows. "I hope my bedroom has one of those."

"Why, how did you guess?" Mr. Colby said in pretend amazement. "And here we thought we'd surprise him, didn't we, Marian?"

"These kids are just too smart for us, I guess," Mrs. Colby answered. She reached down and hauled Mitzi back into the car. "Drive on, Jim. Don't pull into the garage, though. We've got to carry in all the luggage first. Don't anybody go in empty-handed!"

They entered the house through the front door and found themselves in a wide, marble-tiled foyer.

On one side, through an archway, was what was obviously meant to be the dining room. A crystal chandelier hung down in the middle of the room over the spot where a table would normally be placed.

"Grandmother Hammel's old cherrywood china closet ought to look wonderful over there," Mrs. Colby said, pointing to a corner by the front window. "The sun shining in will make the crystal sparkle. This is such a nice, large room. I'll even be able to put the extra leaves in the table and still have plenty of room."

The living room was on the other side of the foyer and had a large fireplace along one wall, with a beautifully carved mantle framing it.

A floor-to-ceiling antique mirror hung over the mantle. It looked old. Early Victorian, at least.

"What a beautiful mirror," Kathy said, staring admiringly at it. "It looks expensive."

Her mother had been hauling her around to

antique auctions for as long as she could remember, so she had a pretty good idea of the price of antiques. That mirror, with its elaborately carved frame and look of opulent old age, must be worth quite a bit.

"It makes the room, doesn't it? Gives it a sort of ambiance," her mother said, waving her hand airily. "My old pieces will look just right in here."

Kathy squinted thoughtfully. "I wonder why they—the former owners—left the mirror behind?"

Her mother didn't answer.

"I mean, it *can* be moved, can't it?"

Still no reply.

Kathy turned to look at her.

Mrs. Colby had a strange expression on her face. Fearful. Guarded. When she became aware of Kathy's gaze, she drew a quick breath and smiled.

"That must have been it," she replied hastily. "Yes, I think the real estate woman might have mentioned it. It . . . the mirror . . . would have been too difficult to pack or something. Now come on, Kathy. I want you and Timothy to see your rooms."

A gently curving staircase led from the foyer up to a long landing that looked down on the entryway.

"There are four bedrooms, two on each side of the landing," Mrs. Colby said.

Timothy stood at the foot of the stairs, looking up. "You said my bedroom has those nice windows that stick out funny, Mommy."

Kathy wished with all her heart that

Timothy wasn't so . . . so dependent. He should have been running around upstairs, looking for his room, instead of standing down here like a timid little mouse, waiting to be led by the hand.

She smothered her feeling of irritation. She shouldn't feel that way about Timmy. It wasn't his fault he was like this. And didn't the doctor say he'd grow out of it?

Feeling guilty for her impatience, she said, "Let's go look at our rooms, shall we, Timmy?"

"They're both to the left of the landing," her mother directed. "Timothy's is the one with the dormer windows that faces out on the street. I thought he'd like the streetlights shining in, since he always wants a little light in his room at night. Yours, Kathy, is the one that overlooks the garden. It has its own adjoining bath."

Kathy gasped with pleasure. "My own bathroom! Why didn't you tell me? You mean I don't have to share with messy old Timmy anymore?"

"No, it's all yours to take long, luxurious bubble baths in. I thought you'd be pleased. That's why I saved it for a surprise."

Kathy and Timothy started up the stairs, Timmy running eagerly a little ahead. Kathy followed at a slower pace, calling encouragement to Mitzi, who trailed behind.

Mitzi, whose arthritic hip always stiffened up after a long ride, was painfully hopping from step to step, favoring her bad hip.

Mitzi had slept in Kathy's room from puppyhood. The family always joked about it, saying that Mitzi probably thought she was Kathy's chaperone, and had to stand guard every night in case some love-crazed boy came climbing in through the window, Romeo-style.

Kathy picked up the old dog and cuddled her protectively in her arms. She kissed Mitzi on the top of her silken little head. The dog was trembling slightly. "Never mind, darling," Kathy soothed. "You'll feel more at home tomorrow. But I'll give you a ride this time, okay?"

When she reached the top of the stairs, she bent over to set Mitzi down on the floor of the landing.

And then the oddest thing happened.

Mitzi suddenly stiffened in her arms and uttered a shrill bark.

Kathy knew it wasn't possible for a dog to cling to a human with its paws, but that was exactly what Mitzi was trying to do. No doubt about it, the little dog didn't want to be put down. At least, not on the landing.

Mitzi's heart was beating loudly, wildly. Kathy could feel it. And the dog's eyes were open and staring, the pupils ringed all around in white, the way they were when she was terribly frightened.

"What on earth is wrong with you, Mitzi?" Kathy asked, puzzled.

She took a step or two backward and sat down on a stair, still holding the trembling dog in her arms.

Mitzi fought her way clear of Kathy's encircling

arms and scuttled down the stairs, her belly close to the ground.

When she reached the foyer, she stood looking up piteously at Kathy and whimpering deep in her throat.

"Dumb dog!" scolded Kathy.

"Come on, Kathy," Timothy called from the landing.

Kathy waggled her finger at the dog. "I'll deal with you later, Miss Twitch."

And then, as she stepped onto the landing, she knew why Mitzi had bolted.

Something was wrong here.

Terribly wrong.

3

The first thing Kathy noticed was the cold.

It was a strange sort of cold. Sudden. Enveloping. Silent. Secret.

Timothy, standing in the hall just a few feet away, was saying something, but his voice seemed distant and distorted.

Around her, the silence deepened and grew more intense, so intense that Kathy could actually hear it, a faint hissing whine, like a television that's just been turned on and is warming up.

And then, briefly, Kathy had the eerie, muffled sensation of being behind a glass wall, one that had just been set beside another glass wall, and that the two walls were rubbing against each other. Rubbing, making contact. Fusing and becoming one.

That's when she felt ... no, *knew* ... that someone was listening. That somehow in that fusing, that blending of space within space, she had tapped into another dimension. Another place. A place where someone, or something was *listening*.

"Kathy!" Timothy's voice broke through the cold, listening silence that surrounded her. "Kathy!"

Suddenly the landing was warm again, and she could hear normal sounds—her parents clattering around downstairs, carrying things in from the car. Mitzi whining in the foyer. A car passing on the street.

"Kathy," Timothy said again, "I've been talking to you and talking to you, and you've just been standing there looking funny!"

Kathy passed a shaking hand over her face.

What happened to me just then? she wondered. Did I pass out or have some sort of fit, or what? I didn't fall down, though. If I'd fainted, I wouldn't have just stood there. I'd have fallen down, wouldn't I?

Crazy, that's what it was. Crazy. Maybe she'd been so tired from the trip that she'd blanked out for a couple of seconds. Fallen asleep on her feet or something. It was possible. She'd read about it once in a Civil War novel, how the soldiers could actually doze while stumbling along on a long march.

Yes, she thought. That's what must have happened to me. I didn't realize I was that tired. Wow!

But what about Mitzi? What spooked Mitzi? And what about that feeling I had when I first stepped on the landing—the feeling that there was something *wrong*?

Mitzi spooks easily. She's even scared of mice.

Maybe she smelled a mouse on the floorboards. Why not? Mom said the house has been standing empty for a while.

But what about you, Kathy? What spooked you? Be honest, now.

Nothing spooked me. I was just tired, that's all. This is the first time I've ever had to move. I'm probably more upset about it than I realize. A traumatic experience, that's what this move has been. No wonder I'm acting dippy.

"Kathy! Listen to me, Kathy! My room's right over here, down the hall. Come look at it with me."

Kathy shook off the last clinging remnants of her waking dream and followed Timothy into his room.

The windows were bare, the blinds raised, and the late afternoon sun shone in, casting long, slanting fingers of light across the room. Dust motes floated and swirled lazily in them.

It was a cozy room, with built-in shelves and cabinets along the shortest wall and a wide closet with a sliding door across the other.

"Why, Timmy, this is a perfect room for a little boy!" Kathy exclaimed, looking around.

Timmy was grinning delightedly. Kathy couldn't remember the last time she'd seen him look so happy. So alive.

She put her arm around his shoulder and together they surveyed the room.

"Those shelves over there will be just right

for your books and model airplanes and those little plastic superhero figures you collect," she told him.

"And the cabinets! You can keep all your games and toys in there, out of sight. Whoever designed this room had a messy little boy in mind, all right."

She gave him a quick hug.

Maybe this move would be good for Timmy after all.

He shrugged her off and ran over to the window. "I want my bed to go right here," he said importantly, thumping the wall. "I want to sit up in bed and look out the window."

He thought for a minute and frowned.

"I wish we could stay here tonight instead of going to some old motel."

"It's only for one night," Kathy explained. "The furniture's coming early tomorrow morning. We'll leave everything here except our toothbrushes. I'll help you unpack your suitcase this afternoon, before we leave. We'll hang up your clothes and then you'll feel like you've already moved in, okay?"

"Well, okay, but we won't sleep too late tomorrow and miss the moving men, will we?" Timothy asked worriedly. "I want to make sure they put my bed and stuff in the right places."

"We won't," Kathy assured him. "You know how hyper Mom's been about her antiques. She's worried they might have gotten scratched and banged in the move. She'll probably have us back here at the crack of dawn."

Timothy wanted to open his suitcase and hang his clothes up right then and there, but Kathy persuaded him to look at the rest of the house with her first.

Her room was larger than his, but it had the same built-in bookcases and cabinets as Timmy's.

The bookcases were large enough to accommodate all her books —she had a collection that went all the way back to her early childhood— and her numerous tapes and CDs.

A mirrored door next to her closet opened into a bathroom. Kathy could hardly wait to see it. Her very own, very private bathroom. What a luxury!

For some reason she'd expected something feminine. Pale pink or rose, maybe. Instead, the tiles were masculine colors, hunter green and beige, and the wallpaper was patterned with brown line-drawings of sailing ships on a cream background.

Oh well, so what. It was hers, all hers. Now if Dad would just spring for a private telephone line . . .

When she came out of the bathroom, Timothy was standing by her windows, looking out.

The windows of her room looked out over the backyard.

Immediately below, she and Timmy could see a large wooden deck with built-in seats. Beyond that, the lot sloped gently downward—wildly overgrown, and dotted with tall, mature trees, clumps of untended azalea and rhododendron bushes, and the unkempt, weedy remains of flower beds gone to seed.

The yard backed onto a dense, heavily wooded area. Tall pine trees stood shoulder-to-shoulder blocking light and view.

Kathy knew they had neighbors on the far side of the woods. She'd seen a map of the town. It was impossible, though, to see any houses through the trees. The privacy would be wonderful after the goldfish-bowl neighborhood they'd just come from.

"Do you think maybe we could plant some flowers out back?" Timothy asked wistfully. "I'll help. I like flowers."

"Maybe, but not until spring," his sister told him. "Besides, it's going to take a lot of work to get that backyard in shape again. Mom and Dad don't like to garden, so maybe they'll live it up and hire professional landscapers to come in and neaten things up for us."

The yard looked so desolate. So abandoned. She shivered a little, looking down on it. Why did she have this feeling of cold and depression? Was she coming down with something?

"This must have been a beautiful yard once," she told Timothy. "It's a shame it's been so neglected."

"Look, Kathy," Timothy said, his little nose flattened against the pane. "What's that?"

"What?"

"Over there." He tapped his finger on the pane. "See? Almost where the woods start."

Kathy squinted in the direction he indicated.

"Oh, Timmy, how nice! We have a fishpond. A little fishpond built of rocks. I wonder why they put it way down there."

"No, Kathy. I mean up in the tree. That big one, just before you get to the fishpond."

He tapped the pane again, and Kathy moved closer to the window.

A huge tree—an oak, by the looks of it— stood at the far end of the lot.

It was very old, judging by its height. Its lowest branch was beyond the grasp of even a tall man. But what was that hanging down from it? A ladder? Yes, that was it. A rope ladder. And up in the fork of the tree was a small, weathered tree house. She could see it clearly now through the gaunt, leafless, November branches.

"It's a tree house, Timmy. An old-fashioned tree house," said Mrs. Colby, coming into the room. "Dad and I wondered how long it would take you to find it. We never thought you'd spot it right away."

Timothy turned from the window, his face glowing with delight. "A tree house? A real tree house like what Tarzan lives in? Whose is it?"

Mrs. Colby laughed and brushed Timothy's hair back from his face. "Why, it's yours, darling. All yours. Your own special place. Daddy went up there when we bought the house and checked to make sure it was safe for you. He knew you'd want to play in it right away."

The look on Timmy's face nearly brought tears to Kathy's eyes. He looked so happy and excited.

I hope this move really *will* be good for him, she thought. Now if he can only find a friend to play with. A real friend, not one of his made up ones.

"Can I go out there right now?" Timmy asked.

"Yes, but maybe Kathy should go with you the first time. I'm a little nervous about your using that ladder."

"I'm a good climber, Mommy. I'll be real careful."

Mrs. Colby turned to Kathy. "You will watch Timmy when he goes up the ladder, won't you? The tree house is so far from the ground. Dad says I'm being silly, that boys Timmy's age do that sort of thing all the time, but still . . . "

Kathy wished her mother wouldn't talk like this in front of Timothy. As if he weren't there, listening. Part of Timmy's problem might be due to Mom's fussing over him all the time and pointing out all the terrible things that could happen to him.

Did she do this to me when I was Timmy's age? Yes, I guess she did, but I was tougher than he is. I did all sorts of stuff that would have given her fits, had she known.

But she mustn't ruin this tree house for Timmy. He's so excited about it. It's time he stopped worrying about hurting himself. Besides, if there are other little boys in the neighborhood, the tree house might lure them into coming over and playing.

In a firm, confident voice, Kathy said, "Will you really let me come see your tree house,

Timothy? But you're going to have to help me up the ladder. I'm not as good a climber as you. You're just like a little monkey."

The look of anxiety that had begun to form on Timothy's face disappeared and he laughed delightedly, puffing up like a baby rooster at her flattery.

"Let's go now, Kathy. I'll show you how good a climber I am."

"But we haven't seen the rest of the upstairs yet," Kathy protested as he seized her hand and began to drag her from the room.

"Aw, we can see all that when we get back," Timmy said.

As they stepped out on the landing, Kathy had a moment of panic.

Would she get that strange feeling again— that feeling of being in some crazy sort of time warp? And the weird sensation that someone was there *listening*?

It was chilly on the landing, but Kathy put that down to the fact that the front door had been left ajar. This was a natural sort of cold. Not that silent, enveloping cold she'd felt before.

No, not felt. Sensed. That was it. Obviously neither Timothy nor her mother had felt anything, so it wasn't physical. It had all been in her mind. A waking dream, that's what it had been, and it would probably never happen again.

It better not, Kathy told herself fiercely as she went down the stairs, her arm around

Timothy. *This is my new home, my beautiful new home, and I'm going to love living in it.*

Yet why couldn't she resist looking back quickly, furtively, over her shoulder at the landing?

4

Timothy loved his tree house.

Over the weekend, while his sister and parents were busy with the unpacking, he spent nearly every waking moment playing in it, sweeping it out and furnishing it with things he'd brought from the house.

When Kathy saw him lugging his sleeping bag and a pair of old cushions down the sloping length of the yard, she offered to help him set up housekeeping. She even volunteered to sew a pair of curtains for the tiny window that overlooked the cracked and abandoned fishpond, but Timothy refused.

"I hope you don't mind," he explained seriously, "but girls aren't 'lowed in my tree house. It's gonna be a clubhouse, just for guys."

Kathy raised her eyebrows at Timmy in mock reproach. "No girls allowed? Shame on you, Timothy Colby." And yet secretly she hoped he *would* find some "guys" willing to share his clubhouse.

"Are you sure Timmy's going to be all right out there by himself?" Mrs. Colby asked her husband. "I mean, you don't think he'll fall off the platform or the rope ladder and hurt himself, do you?"

"He'll be perfectly all right, Marian," Mr. Colby assured her. "And don't you go spooking him, either. Don't point out all the possible ways he can hurt himself. You're going to make a nut case out of the poor kid. You can't keep him wrapped in cotton batting all his life, you know."

"But . . ." Mrs. Colby began.

"Timothy doesn't seem to have a fear of heights," Mr. Colby said. "It's just about the only thing he *isn't* scared of. So if he wants to play up there, more power to him."

Although they worked nonstop all weekend unpacking boxes and trying to get the house in order, Kathy could tell something was bothering her mother. She seemed vague. Distracted. Several times Kathy looked up and found Mrs. Colby watching her speculatively, half-frowning, as if trying to decide whether or not to speak.

Finally, on Sunday, as they were uncrating the last of the good china, Kathy said, "For Pete's sake, Mom, what is it?"

Mrs. Colby widened her eyes in an attempt at innocence. "Why, whatever do you mean?"

"You're transparent as glass, Mom. You act like you're dying to talk to me about something. So talk."

Her mother brushed back her hair with a dusty forearm and sighed. "Well, as a matter of fact, Kathy, there *is* something I think we need to discuss, but this isn't the time. I'd prefer to have Dad in on it when we do. And I'd rather Timothy didn't hear."

"You're making it sound very mysterious, Mom."

"Well it is . . . in a way."

It wasn't until the supper dishes were done and Timothy tucked safely away in bed that Kathy, her mother and her father went into the family room for their long awaited—at least for Kathy—talk.

What could Mom have to say that was so important? Normally she just blurted things out. Why the big buildup?

The family room was one of the first rooms to be put to rights, and already it was beginning to look like home. Cozy. Comfortable. Warm.

The books had all been unpacked and placed in the floor-to-ceiling bookcases that flanked either side of the fireplace. The TV and VCR were set up and ready for action. The down-filled sofa and chairs were arranged invitingly, and the occasional tables had been waxed and buffed and smelled faintly, pleasantly, of lemon oil.

Mrs. Colby snapped on a table lamp while Mr. Colby touched a match to the carefully laid fire in the raised hearth.

The flames sprang up, and soon the fire was going.

Kathy sat cross-legged on the sofa and pulled one of the throw pillows over on her lap. Then she leaned forward, elbows on the pillow, and propped her chin on her hands.

"Okay," she said. "What is it you two wanted to talk to me about? It's kind of late to explain the facts of life, isn't it?"

Mrs. Colby exchanged glances with her husband. He nodded, as if yielding the floor to her.

"It's about the house," Mrs. Colby began. "There's something you should know about it."

Kathy had a strange sense of foreboding. "Does it have anything to do with the fact that the price was so low?"

Mrs. Colby looked over at her husband again and nodded. She cleared her throat. "Remember when I said it was too good to be true? Well, it is."

Kathy sat upright and frowned. "What do you mean? Have they upped the payments on us or something?"

"Oh no, not that," Mrs. Colby said hastily. "But there is something Dad and I thought we should tell you. Something rather upsetting, I'm afraid, about the history of the house. We wanted you to hear it from us, not at school."

"But it's not an old house," Kathy said, puzzled. "How much history can it possibly have?"

Her mother didn't answer at first. She seemed engrossed in running her finger around and around the rim of the coffee mug she was holding.

Mr. Colby coughed discreetly. "Would you rather I told, Marian?"

Kathy looked from one to the other. "Well, somebody better. The suspense is killing me."

Her mother seemed to flinch at the word, "killing."

"No. I will, Jim," she said.

She carefully set her coffee mug down on the table beside her. "It's a long story, Kathy," she began. She hesitated for a moment and then continued. "You see, ten years ago something rather unfortunate happened in this house."

"What do you mean—*unfortunate?*" Kathy demanded.

"Well . . . there was a murder here. More than one murder, actually. Four. A woman and her three children."

"W-H-A-A-T?"

"Please don't shout like that, darling. Let me finish. The original owner of this house was a state department official, just back from an overseas posting. He was extremely well liked and had quite a promising career, from what I've been told. And then, for no apparent reason, he murdered his wife and three sons."

"Here? In this house?"

"Yes. But that's not all. The killer disappeared. He simply dropped out of sight. They couldn't find him. They couldn't trace him. Nothing."

"You mean he was never found?" Kathy asked incredulously. "He murdered his family and ran off. Just like that?"

Mr. Colby cut in. "He had a lot of friends, Kathy. They were all convinced that he probably committed suicide afterward. They reasoned he must have been temporarily insane when he killed his family. This whole thing was so unlike him, they said. He'd always been such a loving husband and father."

Kathy shuddered. "But to murder his own family!"

"That was just it," Mrs. Colby said. "His friends figured that when he realized what he'd done, he must have been so overcome with horror and grief that he took his own life."

"But how would they know that?" Kathy asked. "Who could possibly know something like that?"

"Because the FBI mounted a massive interstate search for him that even extended overseas and involved Interpol," her father told her. "If Charles Winston—that was his name—was still alive, they would have found him."

"And that's why his friends are sure he's dead," put in Mrs. Colby. "And how else but by suicide? He must have been appalled, simply appalled by what he'd done."

"My God," Kathy gasped. "I can't believe something that ghastly could have happened in this house. Right here. A sensational murder where a man killed his own wife and kids."

"Yes," her father replied. "But remember, Kathy, it was a long time ago. Ten years ago."

Kathy couldn't reply. She was afraid she'd

say something she might regret later. Like, why did they wait until they were all moved in to tell her this? She should have been told earlier, and given some say as to whether or not they ought to buy a house with a terrible past like this.

She was aware that her parents were watching her closely. Watching her reactions.

She tried to keep her voice steady and even when she asked, "So has the house stood empty all those years? It didn't look abandoned when we moved in."

"No," her mother hastened to assure her. "It's been kept up. Relatives of the, uh, deceased woman sold the house to a real estate firm and they . . . cleaned it and fixed it up and put it on the market."

"Cleaned it up?" Kathy remembered the red door and her impression of blood. "How did he kill them? Was it messy?"

Her mother's voice was flat and emotionless when she answered. "No. He poisoned them. Perhaps *clean* was the wrong word. *Painted*, then. The real estate firm had the house painted and redecorated."

If I imagined the bloody door, Kathy told herself, then maybe I imagined the rest, too. What happened to me on the landing, I mean.

Aloud she said, "So we aren't the first ones to live here, then, since the murders?" It was a reassuring thought.

Mr. Colby took over. "No. People have come and gone in this house. But I'll be honest with you, Kathy. None of them have stayed for very long."

Again Kathy thought of the upstairs landing and the strange feeling she'd had the first time she set foot on it.

"You're not telling me the house is haunted, are you?" she asked shrilly.

"Of course not," her father replied. "Absolutely not. What nonsense. It's just that most people don't want to live in a house with a past like that."

"And so that's why we were able to buy a house like this for a song," Kathy said bitterly. "We got a murder mansion. Something that no one else wanted."

"Look, Kathy—" her mother began.

"How could you do this?" Kathy demanded, feeling her bitterness turn to anger. "Why would you ever . . . *ever* move us into a house like this?"

"But you like the house. You said you liked the house," her mother protested.

"Like it? Not now. How can I? I'd rather live in a dirty old slum than in a house where some crazy man murdered his very own family!"

"Now you wait just a minute, young lady," Mr. Colby said. "Don't you dare talk to your mother in that tone of voice. Believe it or not, your welfare was the main reason we bought this house."

"My welfare? Are you kidding?"

"You're being hysterical," Mrs. Colby said. "You know perfectly well you're the last person who would ever want to live in a dirty old slum, as you put it."

"I . . ."

"And your father's right. We *were* thinking primarily of you when we bought this house. You're a junior in high school now. You'll be dating and giving parties. We wanted you to have a house you could be proud of, and bring your friends to."

"But there was a murder—*murders*— committed here!"

"Yes," said her mother. "And Dad and I thought about it long and hard. But we finally decided we didn't have much choice. The price of real estate is sky high in the Washington area, as you well know. And with the loss we took when we sold the old house—well, it was either buy this house or rent in a much less desirable neighborhood."

Kathy stole a wistful glance around the comfortable family room. At the expensive wood paneling, the huge stone fireplace and the French doors that led out to the spacious deck.

Her mother eyed her shrewdly, guessing what was passing through her mind, and went on to her closing argument:

"What happened," she said, "happened long, long ago. It's over and done with. Finished. The horror of what took place in this house has been erased by the simple passage of time. Time has a way of doing that, you know."

Mom would have made a terrific trial lawyer, Kathy thought. She has all the right stuff.

Mrs. Colby raised her hand as if she were taking an oath. "This is going to be a happy house. We're going to make it one. After all, houses are only bits of wood, stone and plaster, aren't they? It's the *people* who live in them that make them either happy or unhappy places. And we're going to be happy here, I just know it."

Yes, that's probably the sensible way to look at it, Kathy told herself. Tragedies happen all the time in a lot of places, and yet life goes on and people forget about the horrible things.

Kathy thought about Timothy and his "guys only" tree house. She also thought, with a pleasant sense of curiosity and rising excitement, about her new school and all the kids she was going to meet there.

And what was it Mom had said about giving parties? It would be fun to have a big party here. There was even enough room for dancing, if they spilled out onto the deck.

She could almost see it now. Japanese lanterns and couples slow-dancing to dreamy music. And her, with some really hunky guy. Beth said she was going to meet someone really hunky.

"Yes," Kathy said, after a pause. "Yes. I guess you're right, Mom. It *would* be wrong to spoil everything by dwelling on something that happened a long time ago."

Still . . . for a second she was tempted to tell her parents about her strange experience on the landing.

No, that would be a mistake. They would think she'd flipped her lid and probably send her to a psychologist.

"Well, thank God that's settled," Mr. Colby said, reaching for the remote control and clicking on the TV. "Now how about you girls letting me watch a good Western, for a change?"

5

It happened again that night.

Kathy awoke to the sound of a dog barking.

At first she thought it was Mitzi. The little dog had refused, in spite of much coaxing, to climb the stairs at bedtime. She'd stood at the foot of the staircase and whimpered, but wouldn't follow, even though Kathy tempted her with a doggie treat. Finally, Kathy had fixed her a bed in a corner of the kitchen.

"It's those stairs," Mrs. Colby said, shaking her head. "I'm afraid they're simply too much for poor old Mitzi. "I wish there was something we could do about her arthritis."

No, you're wrong, Kathy thought. It's not the stairs that bother Mitzi. It's what lies at the top of the stairs. Dogs have a sixth sense about these things.

The landing. That cold, silent landing. There's something wrong with it. Something weird is going on there. I'm almost sure of it now, but only Mitzi feels what I do.

The dog sounded distressed. It would bark shrilly and then whimper piteously. A brief silence, and then it would start all over again. It was the same every time. Almost like a recording. The barking and then the whimpering.

Was Mitzi, down in the kitchen, making all that noise? Maybe she was confused by her strange surroundings.

Kathy got out of bed and slipped into her bathrobe. She was preparing to open her bedroom door when the barking began again.

No. Those barks weren't coming from the kitchen. That dog was out in the backyard.

Had Mitzi gotten outside? But how had she managed to do that? Kathy's parents always locked the house up tight as a drum every night. Kathy went to her window and peered out over the long, sloping lawn.

It was a night of a full moon. The yard was lit up clearly by an eerie wash of pale yellow light. She couldn't see any movement out there.

The dog barked again. Closer this time. There was a more desperate, more urgent note in his voice now.

No, that definitely wasn't Mitzi. Maybe it was a stray. Or maybe a neighbor's dog had gotten loose. But where was it?

Wait a minute. It sounded like it was right below her window now. She still couldn't see it, but she could hear the keening and moaning.

What on earth was the matter with that poor thing?

Kathy raised the window and pressed her forehead against the screen.

Nothing. There was nothing down there. Surely she would be able to see a dog at this short distance with the moon as bright as it was.

She unhooked the bottom latch of the screen and pushed it out so that she could hang over the window sill and look down.

Still nothing. And the whimpering and moaning had stopped. Had he run off, or was he lying in the bushes? Maybe he was sick.

She was surprised the dog hadn't roused her mother. Mrs. Colby was a notoriously light sleeper. She must be pretty tired from the unpacking, Kathy thought, to sleep through all this.

She went over to her door, moving as quietly as possible, opened it and tiptoed out into the hall. No sense waking up the whole household. Maybe she was making too big a thing of this. Maybe the dog had realized he was at the wrong house and had simply run off.

Up ahead, the landing was a pool of darkness. She would have to grope her way to the stairs, but then she'd be okay. The moonlight, slanting in through the fan-shaped window over the front door, illuminated the steps.

Kathy felt the cold the minute she set foot on the landing. It was the bitter, bone chilling cold she'd felt the day before.

For a moment she stood there, unable to move. She could feel the hairs on the back of her neck begin to rise, like a frightened cat's.

Why was she standing here, glued to the spot? Was she afraid of . . . disturbing . . . whatever was there on the landing?

Could this whole thing be merely a product of her wild imagination?

She took a deep breath. "Is anybody there?" she whispered.

No reply. But Kathy had the distinct impression that someone—or something—heard her. That it was listening to her.

The silence was almost palpable. Again, as she had the day before, she felt she could actually *hear* the silence, that high-pitched, faintly hissing sound, like electronic equipment warming up. And again she had the terrifying feeling that she was not alone. That there was a *presence* up here. That was the only word for it. The only word that described what she sensed there on the landing. A *presence*—the cold, and that strange, listening stillness.

Clutching her bathrobe closer about her, Kathy made her way as quickly as possible across the darkened landing and ran down the stairs.

Now she was in the foyer. It was warm there. Normal. Safe.

She stood for a moment, looking up. Had that weird thing really happened to her again? It suddenly seemed unbelievable that just a few seconds ago she'd almost been paralyzed with cold and fear.

Was she cracking up or what? This was unreal. Things like this only happened in science fiction thrillers. Maybe that something "wrong" about the foyer was only in her head, after all.

A whimper from the kitchen roused her.

Mitzi. She'd check on her first, and then go out into the backyard and try to find that other dog.

When she snapped on the overhead light in the kitchen, Mitzi was nowhere to be seen. Her doggie bed by the broom closet was empty.

Then Kathy heard another whimper. It came from behind a stack of packing boxes in the corner.

"Why, Mitzi," Kathy said, pushing the boxes aside and picking up the little dog. "Now what's wrong? What are you hiding from?"

Mitzi was trembling again, the way she had on the landing the previous day. Her eyes looked wild, too.

Kathy perched on a kitchen chair and began to rock Mitzi. She could feel the trembling gradually subsiding.

"Did you have a bad dream, Mitzi?" she asked gently. "Is that what scared you?"

Mitzi squirmed around, trying to find a more comfortable spot in Kathy's arms.

"Or was it the barking outside?" Kathy stood up, still holding Mitzi. "Do you want to help me find that dog and see if he's okay?"

When Kathy opened the back door, Mitzi began to wriggle frantically, indicating she wanted down. Her short legs started moving the minute they hit the floor, and she ran back to her corner and crawled behind the packing boxes again.

"All right, then," Kathy said. "If that's how you feel, I'll go by myself."

Taking a flashlight from the shelf beside the door, she went out into the night, snapping on the outdoor lights.

She whistled tentatively a couple of times and listened for a reply as she shone her light around the deck and the surrounding lawn.

No answering bark or whimper, except from Mitzi, back in the kitchen.

Kathy walked out a little farther into the yard and turned slowly, playing the beam of her flashlight around her. Again, nothing. If there'd been a dog out here before, he was certainly gone now.

She went back into the kitchen, locking the door securely behind her and fastening the chain. "Are you okay now, Mitzi?" she called in the direction of the packing boxes. "If it was that dog's barking that scared you, you can relax. He's gone now."

Kathy kept the flashlight with her as she made her way back to the foyer and up the stairs.

She stopped one step short of the landing and flashed the light around.

It certainly looked innocent enough up there. No spooks. No goblins.

Mrs. Colby had set a long, narrow antique side table against the wall at the top of the steps and had placed tall pewter candlesticks on either end with a Chinese porcelain bowl in the direct center. Kathy had always liked that table.

She'd played under it when she was small. The sight of it bolstered her courage.

Just three or four steps, she told herself, five at the most, and I'm across the landing and safe in the hallway.

And yet her feet refused to move.

She couldn't feel the cold here. That only hit when she actually stood on the landing itself. There was no hint of it here, on this step.

Maybe *it* wouldn't happen this time.

She stepped up on the landing.

And froze.

It was colder now, if possible, than ever before, and the hiss of the silence was louder. It seemed to swirl around her, like a mist. And in that hissing, she was sure she could hear whispers—desperate, intense, whispers—but she couldn't tell what it was they were saying.

And then she felt something furry brush up against her.

And heard a whimper. The soft whimper of a frightened dog.

Kathy opened her mouth to scream, but no sound came out.

And then she thought, *Mitzi!* Mitzi followed me upstairs!

She shone the flashlight around the landing. She was trembling so violently that the light fluttered and wavered over the walls and floor.

Nothing. She was alone on the landing.

The whispers had ceased, but the cold—the penetrating, bone-chilling cold—still remained.

"Mitzi?" she called out softly.

A distant *yip* came in answer from the kitchen.

And another faint whimper from the landing beside her.

Kathy dropped the flashlight and ran toward her parents' room, stumbling in the dark and hitting the antique table with her hip as she passed. One of the candlesticks fell with a clatter to the floor and rolled around noisily.

Mrs. Colby was snapping on the bedside light as Kathy burst through the door.

"Kathy!" she cried. "What's wrong?"

"There . . . there's something on the landing!" Kathy managed to gasp, slamming the door behind her. "Something awful!"

Mr. Colby leapt out of bed, not stopping to put on his robe, and headed for the door.

"Wait, Jim!" Mrs. Colby cried, throwing back the covers and following him. She grabbed him by the sleeve of his pajamas. "Stay here. We'll call the police."

Mr. Colby held up his hand for silence.

"Who's out there, Kathy?" he whispered. "Did you get a good look at him?"

"N . . . no," Kathy stammered. "I couldn't see anything, but I think it's a dog."

"A *dog*?" Mr. Colby said incredulously, no longer whispering. "There's a *dog* on our landing? Are you sure?"

"Yes. I could feel its fur. I could hear it."

Mrs. Colby put her palm on Kathy's head. "Are you sick? Do you have a fever?"

Kathy pushed her mother's hand away impatiently. "No. I went downstairs to the kitchen and when I came back up, there it was."

Mr. Colby opened the door cautiously and peeped out. Then he reached his arm around the door frame and felt along the wall for the hall light switch.

The hall and foyer came alive with light. Mr. Colby stepped out of the doorway and looked around. Then he went down the hall to the landing.

"There's nothing up here, Kathy," he called

back. He walked over to the railing and looked down on the foyer. "And there's nothing down there, either."

Kathy and her mother ventured out on the landing. Mrs. Colby stooped over and picked up the fallen pewter candlestick. She looked at Kathy skeptically. "Are you sure you weren't having a nightmare, darling?"

The look on her face told Kathy that her mother thought this was merely a figment of Kathy's wild, midnight imagination.

Well, no wonder. The landing looked so harmless. The cold had gone away. It was cozy and pleasant and warm now.

"No, it wasn't a nightmare," Kathy protested. "I think—I'm sure—it was a dog. It was furry. I *felt* it, Mom."

"What do you mean—you *think* it was a dog? Didn't you see it?" her father asked.

"Well . . . no. The light wasn't on. It was dark up here."

Mr. Colby picked up the flashlight Kathy had dropped in her panic.

"But you had a flashlight, obviously."

"That's the scary part, Dad. I felt the dog and I could hear him. But I couldn't see him, even with the flashlight."

"You couldn't see him?" her father asked. "He was there but you couldn't *see* him?"

"Yes, I know it sounds crazy, but . . . "

Her parents exchanged a long look. "Well," Mr. Colby said at last. "I'd better check the house. We'll all sleep better if I do."

"But there *was* a dog! I swear it!" Kathy said, close to tears.

"Maybe a window was left open somewhere and he got in," her father said tightly. "And maybe he went out the same way."

She knew her father didn't believe that. He was only saying it to calm her down.

He went down the stairs, his bare feet making slap-slapping sounds on the wooden treads.

Mrs. Colby put her arm around Kathy. "I'll put you to bed and stay with you until Dad comes back."

Kathy suddenly remembered an old Irish folk tale she'd read once about a ghostly dog barking under a window to announce an approaching death.

That dog outside—she wasn't able to see him, either.

And then, on the landing . . .

Was it the same dog?

And where was Timmy? Why hadn't he come out of his room to see what all the excitement was about?

Could it be that Timmy . . . ?

"Wait a minute, Mom," she said, her heart giving a lurch. "Let's look in on Timmy. I'm surprised he slept through all the noise."

The moonlight shone full upon Timmy in his bed next to the window. Kathy could see his chest moving up and down and hear his deep breathing. He stirred slightly and then rolled over on one side.

Timmy was okay. Well, of course he would be.

What was happening to her? Why on earth did she think he might be in some sort of danger?

Her mother was looking fondly down on the little boy. He looked even smaller and paler asleep in the moonlight than he did by day. The inherited Colby flaxen blonde hair that was so striking on Kathy only seemed to make Timothy look washed-out and frail. And now, in this moonlight, he looked like a marble angel.

As they came out into the hall again, Mr. Colby was waiting for them.

"There's no sign of a dog, Kathy," he said. "And all the windows and doors are locked up tight."

"But I couldn't have imagined it, Dad?" Kathy protested. "How could I? I felt its fur and—"

Mr. Colby grinned. "Maybe this is what you felt." He held up Mrs. Colby's lambswool cardigan. "I found it draped over the banister on the landing. You must have brushed up against it in the dark and panicked."

Kathy ran her hand over it. Yes, it was soft and furry, like a dog. "But I heard the dog, Dad. I heard it whimper."

"That could have been any number of things," he told her. "A sound outside. Or maybe Timmy made a noise in his sleep."

He rubbed his eyes wearily. "You've spooked yourself, that's all," he said. "Now that you know a murder was committed in this house, your imagination has kicked into high gear."

"But what if I'm *not* imagining it?"

She remembered Timmy and lowered her voice. "I haven't wanted to say anything about this before, Dad. I was afraid you'd think I was crazy. But this isn't the first time something weird has happened to me on this landing."

"What do you mean, *weird*?" Mrs. Colby asked.

"I've felt a funny sort of cold up here twice before. You know, like you read about in ghost stories—those freezing spots in rooms where there's been a murder or suicide. And when I felt that weird cold, I got the feeling that—I'm not imagining this, Mom!—the feeling that, well, somebody's here . . . listening."

"What on earth are you talking about?" Mrs. Colby demanded. "Who's up here? And what are they listening *for*?"

"I don't know. I can't see them. I just sort of *feel* that they're there."

Mrs. Colby threw up her hands. "Really, Kathy, this is all perfectly ridiculous! You spend too much time reading trashy horror novels. Trust me, this landing definitely is *not* inhabited by ghosts. Or by little green men from outer space. And it's no colder than any other spot in the house. Right, Jim?"

Mr. Colby nodded. "Your mother's right, Kathy. There's nothing wrong with this house. Not now, anyway. And maybe you ought to try reading something besides tales of the supernatural for a change."

"Honestly, Dad," Kathy protested. "You know perfectly well I don't just read . . . "

Her voice trailed away as a thought came to her. "Read! That's it. Those murders must have been on the front pages of the local paper for weeks. They're bound to have old copies at the library. I can find out exactly what *did* happen in this house. And where."

"No, Kathy," her mother said. "Don't. Please."

"But Mom—why not?"

"Because you'll make a nervous wreck of yourself if you do. You're too imaginative. You'll fill your head with the images of the murder . . . murders . . . that took place in our house, and we'll have scenes like this every night."

"But—"

"No, Kathy. Let it go. Give the house a chance. Besides, if you walk around here spooked, Timmy's going to pick up on it and then we'll really have problems."

"I . . . I guess you're right, Mom."

Mr. Colby started down the hall toward his room, then turned. "Maybe you shouldn't go running around in the dark, Kathy, until you're more used to the house. This move has been hard on you. It's been hard on all of us. So let's all go back to bed. I'm bushed."

"Yes, darling," Mrs. Colby said, brushing a quick kiss across Kathy's forehead. "That's probably it. You're simply a little overwrought about the move. We'll talk more about it in the morning."

As Kathy climbed back into bed she thought, *I couldn't have imagined all that. Could I? There was a dog out back, I'm sure of it. And I was sure there was one on the landing. I felt it touch me.*

Well, maybe it *was* Mom's old cardigan all along. And maybe the whimper she'd heard had been Timothy. Or a sound from outside. She'd better get a grip or next she'd be walking around talking to herself.

But I could swear that whimper came from right next to me. Give me a logical explanation for that one, Dad.

No. Mustn't think about that now.

She turned off the light and forced herself to relax. Tomorrow was her first day of school at Brentwood High. She didn't want to show up looking like death warmed over.

And yet she couldn't explain away the feeling she got on the landing.

The cold. The hissing silence.

"Please, please," she prayed, "don't let it have anything to do with the murders that took place in this house."

7

The man waited until the last light went off
in the house before he slipped back into the
woods.

He'd seen the moving van arrive Friday. He'd
dared not loiter to see what was being carried
into the house. His house. Someone might see
him watching and wonder at his curiosity.

He came back tonight because The Voices
told him to. Sometimes they told him to do things
he didn't understand. But that was all right. The
time would come when everything would be made
clear to him, they said.

He'd almost come out of the woods, though,
when he heard the dog barking and whining. At
first he'd thought it was Roxie. It sounded just
like her. But how could that be? The dog had
been gone for ten years.

And then he'd had another shock. The girl.
The girl with the long blonde hair. When she
came outside and stood there with the light shining on her hair, she looked like Estelle.

No, not Estelle as he'd known her, but as Estelle must have looked as a teenager. That same pale hair. Storybook hair, he'd always called it, like the princesses who lived in ivory towers had. And for one brief, heart-stopping moment, he'd even thought that maybe it was the ghost of Estelle, made young by death, come to haunt him.

And then she had turned and he'd seen to his relief that it wasn't Estelle. It was just the hair that was the same.

The man shook his head roughly, as a dog might. Sometimes things felt loose and disconnected up there in his brain. Shaking his head made it feel better.

Still shaking his head, he made his way through the woods, toward the back street where his van was parked.

Coming in midterm to a strange school wasn't as frightening as Kathy had thought it would be.

Brentwood High was a pleasant surprise. It was smaller than her old school. More personal. Almost like a private school. And it was newer and better designed. The classrooms were open and sunny and well equipped.

Best of all, the kids seemed friendly.

She'd worried a lot about that, wondering whether they would accept her, or even realize she was alive.

Maybe nobody will speak to me, she'd thought desperately.

Instead, one of the senior girls had been waiting for her at the front door.

"Are you Kathy?" she asked. "I'm Maureen. Maureen Sullivan. Mr. Ericson—he's the principal—asked me to show you around."

Maureen was short, red-haired and freckled with a sunny smile. She seemed to know everyone in school. She piloted Kathy through the halls, stopping every now and then to introduce her.

"The reason Mr. Ericson picked me was because I'm new here, too. Sort of. I've only been here about a month," she said, as they threaded their way toward the principal's office.

"You? I thought you've probably been here forever," Kathy said incredulously. "You know so many people."

"That's the nice thing about Brentwood High," Maureen told her. "Most of the kids' parents are either in the military, the foreign service or some government agency. We've all moved around a lot. Always been the new kids on the block, so to speak. When you grow up like that, you learn how to make friends fast."

She stopped in front of the glass-fronted principal's office. "Okay, here we are. The secretary's name is Ms. Wolff. She'll give you your schedule and point you toward your homeroom. I'll check back with you later, to see how things are going. In the meantime," she paused and pointed to her flaming hair, "I'm easy to spot in a crowd, so if you need me, just whistle."

"Ms. Wolff gave Kathy her class schedule and ushered her into the principal's office.

Mr. Ericson, square built and slightly balding, rose from his chair with a pleasant smile.

"Welcome to Brentwood High, Kathy," he said. "I'll make this brief because the first bell is about to ring. Your transfer grades are good. No problems there. Our curriculum is basically the same as in your old school, so you ought to adapt easily without falling behind or losing any ground."

The first bell rang and there was a mass shuffling in the halls as the students all headed for their homerooms.

"Oh, and one other thing," Mr. Ericson said as Kathy left. "We have some wonderful extracurricular activities at this school. I hope you'll sign up for at least one of them. Ms. Wolff will give you a complete list."

Kathy was the last to enter her homeroom, and she felt everyone's eyes on her. She hadn't known what to wear that morning—did they get dressed up here, or was it strictly jeansville? So she'd tried to play it down the middle with a denim mini skirt, black tights and a black turtleneck.

She knew she looked good in black, with her long, silver-blonde hair.

And she knew she was pretty—or at least that people thought of her as pretty. Not beautiful, exactly, but pretty. Pretty enough, anyway.

Some of the girls were looking at her speculatively, probably wondering if she was going to be witchy or stuck-up. Well, they'd find out soon enough that she wasn't.

A couple of guys were regarding her with open admiration. That happened sometimes. It was her hair. When she wore it straight and hanging down her back like this, boys seemed to notice her in a big way.

Ms. Young, her homeroom teacher, introduced her to the class and waved her to the only empty seat. It was in the rear, and she had to walk the entire length of the classroom to get there. It seemed to take forever. She could feel the color rising in her cheeks as she made her way past a living gauntlet of jutting elbows and legs to her seat.

She was greeted by a low whistle as she passed one row, followed by some theatrical heavy breathing.

A dark-haired girl in the end seat shook her head sympathetically and murmured, "These guys are total animals. Ignore them."

"Amen to that," said the girl sitting next to her.

Kathy crawled over legs to her appointed seat and sank back with a sigh of relief. She would have loved to fan herself, but that might have been a little too obvious.

"Welcome to Brentwood High," whispered a voice in her ear.

She looked. And then she looked again.

There he was. The hunk Beth had promised she would meet. Sandy hair. Grey eyes. An impressive set of shoulders.

No, this can't be. This isn't one of those afternoon soap operas. Things like this just don't happen to me. There has to be something wrong with him. Maybe he picks his nose and moves his lips when he reads. Or has wet palms.

Then again, maybe Beth is a gypsy fortune teller. Don't I wish!

The hunk scribbled something in his note-book and turned it toward her:

"I need to talk to you," the note said. "Hang around a minute after the bell, okay?"

Kathy nodded mutely. She even liked his handwriting. Small but not cramped. Neat but masculine. Efficient looking. Yes, definitely efficient looking.

Wow! What's happening here?

Do all the boys at Brentwood High come on this fast?

Wait a minute, she told herself sternly. If something seems too good to be true, it probably is.

She looked sideways, suspiciously at him, her eyes narrowed. He smiled back innocently. Nice teeth.

Maybe he was one of those good looking, charming, user types. The kind who think that girls are put on earth for their convenience. She'd met a couple of them before.

That would explain the quick pick-up approach. Those guys seemed to assume that all they had to do was turn on the charm and the girls would come running. He probably wanted to be the first guy in school to date the new blonde. Well, he was in for a big surprise!

When the bell rang, she gathered up her new notebooks and prepared to leave, but he laid a detaining hand on her arm.

"Wait a minute. We have to talk. Remember?" he said.

"I don't want to be late for my next class," she said coolly. "Maybe another time."

"This will only take a minute," he replied. "By the way, my name's Matt. Matt Hamilton."

She inclined her head slightly.

"Anyway," he went on, "I know this is kind of sudden, but I wanted to sign you up before anyone else got you."

"I *beg* your pardon?" she said, drawing herself up to her full height. "I don't have the slightest idea what you mean."

"Oh, sorry," he said, and blushed. He shook his head. "You must think I'm some kind of nut. What I mean is, I saw that you're carrying a list of extracurricular activities, and I thought—I hoped, anyway—that you might be looking for an interesting group to join. And, well, we sure could use you. We're pretty shorthanded at the *Bugle*."

"You mean the school band?" Kathy said. "I'm sorry but I don't play a musical instrument."

"No. I mean the school paper. The *Brentwood Bugle*." He shrugged helplessly. "It's a terrible name, but we can't change it. We've tried."

Now it was Kathy's turn to feel like a fool. So he'd been harmless all along!

"Are you the editor?"

"No. That's Mel Kramer. He's a senior. I'm the assistant editor."

"Look . . . uh . . . Matt. I've really got to go."

"Where's your next class?"

Kathy consulted her schedule card. "Room 206. English. I'm not sure I know where it is."

"I do. I'm right next door to you. Social Studies. We can talk as we walk."

They shouldered their way through the crowded corridors. "As I was saying," he went on, "we need some additional writers for the features department."

Kathy stopped walking. "Wait a minute. How do you know I can write?"

He blushed again. "I can tell. You look like a journalist. Am I right or am I right?"

"I guess you're right," Kathy admitted. "English is my best subject. And I was on the school paper back home—I mean, at my old high school."

They resumed walking. "But if you're that desperate for writers," she said, "I'll bet you were ready to sign me up even if I'd never worked on a paper before. Am I right or am I right?"

"You're right," he said with a wry smile. "Touché. But it looks like the *Bugle* got lucky. Well, here's your room. By the way, when's your lunch period?"

She studied her schedule card again. "Eleven-thirty. Why?"

"So's mine. Why don't you join us journalists at our regular table? Left side, in front of the third window."

"Well . . . all right."

"We like to think of ourselves as kind of different, you know?" said a thin, intense girl named Jassy, leaning over the cafeteria table at Kathy.

"Like those New York writers in the '30s who used to meet all the time at the Algonquin hotel. Talented. Artistic."

"Jassy believes in tooting her own *horn*," said a boy named Chip.

Everyone laughed immoderately.

Matt had related the story of how, when he told Kathy they were shorthanded at the *Bugle*, she'd asked, "You mean the school band?" And now they were all vying with each other to see who could bring the most names of musical instruments into the group conversation.

Even Kathy thought it was funny. As Matt said, "We're not laughing at you, Kathy. It's just that we hate the name of the paper. It really *does* sound more like a marching band than a campus periodical, doesn't it?"

"Well, I don't mean to *harp* on this," said Hank Irving, one of the feature writers, "but we really need some new ideas for the feature page. Otherwise, our circulation is going to go down the tubes. Excuse me, I meant *tubas*."

More laughter mixed with a few groans.

"Maybe Kathy can suggest something her old school paper did to increase circulation," said Matt. "Some sort of column to spark a little reader interest."

"Yeah," Chip said. "To cast a net over our readers. *Castanet*. Get it?"

"Quit *horning* in, Chip," Hank told him.

The bell for fifth period rang.

"Saved by the *bell*," Matt said, raising his

eyebrows at Kathy. "The group isn't usually this hard to handle."

"So what do you think of the staff of the *Bugle*, Kathy?" Chip asked.

She opened her eyes wide and fluttered her lashes, the very picture of the mythical "dumb blonde." "I don't know. I don't play a musical instrument."

That night, lying in bed, Kathy looked back on the day with satisfaction.

She hadn't felt that awful, cold silence on the landing today. After last night, she'd been afraid that . . . But it hadn't.

Maybe her worries about starting a new school had made her slightly whacko. Given her weird delusions. Yes, that was probably it. And didn't Mom always accuse her of having an overactive imagination?

Well, she was ready to get on with her new life now.

She liked the kids she'd met. Maureen Sullivan, the helpful senior. Everybody on the staff of the *Bugle*. If they were an example of the rest of the student body, she wasn't going to have any trouble settling in here at Brentwood High.

Yes, she missed her old friends, but, as Beth said, sometimes you have to move on.

She especially liked Matt Hamilton. She'd have to write Beth about him. And to think that at first she'd had him pegged for a pick-up artist!

She blushed in the dark, remembering. Well, he'd never know anything about that, thank heaven.

All in all, it had been a pretty good day.

Maybe she was going to like it here after all.

Kathy telephoned Beth that weekend. It would eat up most of her allowance, but it would be worth it. She had too many things to tell her old friend. It would take too long to get it all down on paper.

"It sounds like everything turned out okay, after all," Beth said when Kathy finally ran out of breath. "I told you it would, remember?"

"Yes, but I wish you were closer," Kathy told her. "I really miss you, Beth."

"Keep the good thought," Beth replied cheerfully. "I just might be parked on your doorstep one of these days. Dad's overdue for Pentagon duty and Mom's already starting to moan about having to move. But by the time I get there, you and that hunk, Matt, will probably be voted the couple of the year, and you won't have any time left over for me."

"Oh yeah?" Kathy said. "Try me. Besides, Matt and I are only friends. We work on the paper together, but that's it. He hasn't even asked me out yet."

"He will. Honestly, Kathy, you've got a lot more sex appeal than you realize. By the way, how's Timmy doing?"

"Not too well." Kathy carried the telephone into the hall closet and closed the door, in case Timmy was hanging around. "He really likes the house, but it's the same old story at school. He just never makes any friends. But we've got this tree house in our backyard and he plays in it all the time. I keep hoping that eventually some of the neighborhood kids will come over and want to play up there with him."

"Don't worry, Kathy. It's only a matter of time before Timothy makes friends. Some kids are just slow starters . . . "

But as the days passed, Timothy spent more and more time playing alone in his tree house in the overgrown area of the garden down by the woods.

The tree house was built on a platform set high in the branches of the tall oak tree. Timmy always used the rope ladder to climb up to it, since the lowest branches of the tree were too high to grasp, even by an adult.

Mrs. Colby had stopped worrying about him falling. She'd watched him climb the ladder several times and was reassured to see how nimble and sure-footed he was.

Winter was coming. It was colder now, and starting to get dark early.

"Where's Timmy?" Kathy asked one evening, coming into the kitchen.

Mrs. Colby shrugged. "Guess."

"You mean, he's still up in his tree house?" Kathy asked incredulously.

"It's so cold out there. And it will be dark soon."

"I'll call him in just a minute, but first there's something you should know, Kathy."

Mrs. Colby wiped her hands on a tea towel and sat down at the kitchen table. "Dad and I have been giving some serious thought to sending Timmy to a child psychologist."

Kathy sat down across from her mother. "Do you really think his problems are that bad, Mom?"

"It's not that he has problems, exactly," Mrs. Colby said. She drew a deep breath and let it out slowly. "It's just that we'd like to avert one. We'd like to find out why he isn't relating to other children."

"But Mom," Kathy protested. "Maybe he won't be that way much longer. You always said I was shy when I was little."

"Yes, but not *that* shy. And you'd outgrown it by the time you were his age. It's time he outgrew it, too, and started to make real friends at school. He's getting too old for those imaginary ones he keeps coming up with."

"And you think a child psychologist can help him?" Kathy asked.

"Well, it's a start, anyway." She got up from the table. "And now I'd better go call your brother before he freezes to death out there."

Timothy came in, his cheeks red from the

cold. He took off his jacket and, standing on tip-toe, hung it on the rack by the back door.

Then he walked over to the table and sat down, hooking his heels over the footrail of the chair and resting his chin on his hands.

"Is this a bad house, Mommy?" he asked.

Mrs. Colby was at the sink, scraping carrots. She turned quickly, her eyes wide. "Why, Timmy, what do you mean?"

"I mean, did something awful happen here?"

Mrs. Colby shot Kathy a warning glance. The message was clear.

Timmy mustn't be told about the murders!

"Who said something awful happened here?" Kathy asked cautiously.

"A kid at school," Timothy said. "He said somebody died in this house."

His mother laid down her paring knife. "People *do* die in houses, Timmy," she said, choosing her words carefully. "They don't always die in hospitals. Grandpa Hammel died in Grandma's old house, remember?"

Timmy nodded. "I liked that house."

"Of course you did. You never thought there was anything bad or awful about it, did you?"

Timmy shook his head vigorously, his pale-blonde hair flying. "No. It always smelled good. Like cookies. "

"That was because Grandma Hammel liked to bake," Mrs. Colby said.

"And after Grandpa died, did she ever tell you she didn't like the house anymore?"

"N . . . no," Timmy said thoughtfully, remembering. "She said she had nice memories of Grandpa in every single room."

"That's right. That's just how Grandma felt about her house," Mrs. Colby said, picking up her paring knife again. "And now I'll answer your question. Yes, Timmy, people have died in this house. But we didn't know them, so we will never have any memories of them, good or bad. Okay?"

"That's kind of what Philip said," Timmy said.

"Philip?" Kathy asked sharply. "Is he the boy who told you about the house?"

"No, that was Brian." Timmy made a face. "He's not nice. The teacher made him sit in the hall today."

"So who's Philip?" Mrs. Colby asked.

"He's my friend. He came and played with me today in the tree house."

Kathy and her mother exchanged triumphant glances.

"Why, Timmy! I'm so glad you've made a friend! Where does he live?" asked Mrs. Colby.

"Over there somewhere, I think," Timothy replied with a vague wave of his arm toward the backyard.

"You mean on the street behind the woods?" Kathy asked.

Timmy looked blank. "I guess so. I was up in the tree house and when I looked out, there he was, standing by the fishpond."

He chuckled. "He's just like me. He's as old as me and he looks like me. He even has hair the same color as mine. And he loves my tree house. He says it's his most favorite place in the whole world."

Kathy got up and started setting the table. "I hope we can meet him soon, Timmy."

"I don't know," Timmy said, looking away. "He's kind of shy. Can I watch TV before supper, Mom?"

"For a little while. But go wash up first," his mother replied.

"So what do you think, Mom?" Kathy asked when Timmy had left the room.

"I have to admit, he had me going there for a minute, Kathy," her mother said. "But I'm afraid it's only another of his imaginary friends."

"We can't be sure, though," Kathy put in hurriedly. "Maybe Philip is real."

Mrs. Colby opened the oven door and peered in at the roast.

"Don't I wish. But no, Philip has all the earmarks of one of Timmy's imaginary friends." She shut the door with a sigh and straightened up, her hands on her hips. "Timmy says they're the same age. And that Philip looks like him. Even has the same color hair. And—this is the giveaway, Kathy—they like the same things. Philip's favorite place is the tree house, Timmy says. What a coincidence. Timmy's been obsessed with that tree house ever since we got here."

"I guess you're right," Kathy said. "He said he doesn't know where Philip lives, either. He said Philip just showed up by the fishpond. Do you think he really *sees* these kids, Mom?"

"I guess so," her mother said. "I'm convinced

now that we should take Timmy to a psychologist. It's high time he came into the real world."

Kathy drifted over to the window and looked out, down the long stretch of back lawn. It had been misty and rainy all day, and now, with dusk coming on, the oak tree and the fishpond were shrouded in a delicate, cobwebby fog.

With a little imagination, she thought, even I could mistake that faint, misty patch down there by the woods for a little boy.

A small, beckoning boy with pale, silvery-blonde hair.

The Voices had told the man to come back *again tonight.*

Something was wrong—terribly wrong here.

This afternoon, when he'd been hiding in the woods, he'd seen Philip playing in the old tree house. Yes, he was sure it was Philip.

What was Philip doing here?

Why wasn't he with the others?

He was supposed to be with the others. It was all part of The Great Plan.

And now, here he was again. Had he come back, or had he never . . . left?

He would have to figure out why Philip was here and what to do about it. Maybe They would help him.

But now, tonight, he would see what he could find out about the people who were living in his house.

Who were they? What claim did they have on the house?

The Voices refused to answer him when he

asked about these people. Maybe it was a test. Yes, that must be it. The Voices were testing him to see if he was worthy of the responsibility they had given him.

He crept forward across the lawn, a ghostly figure in the faint, wavering light of the moon. A moving shadow. If anyone looked out of a window now, they wouldn't see him. He'd learned, long ago, how to be somewhere and yet not be seen.

He was behind the large holly bush now, at the edge of the deck. He'd planted that bush many years ago. He and Estelle. Her long, fair hair had been tied up in a bandanna, and she'd laughed when she pricked her finger on the sharp leaf of the holly.

"Now I really do feel like one of those fairy tale princesses you're always comparing me to," she said. "The one who pricked her finger and fell into an enchanted sleep for one hundred years. Tell me, Charles, would you cut your way through the brambles that surrounded me to awaken me with a kiss?"

"Yes," he'd said. "Oh yes."

How he'd loved her. He still did. It was a perfect love. That's why They selected him, coming to him, faintly at first, and then louder, more insistent, with their demands. Their demands for a perfect sacrifice.

He looked up at one of the upstairs windows. That was where the pale-haired girl slept. The one whom he had mistaken, at first, for a young Estelle. He'd seen her through the window that other night.

He glanced around. If he really wanted to, he could climb up the trellis and enter her room. The window was open and that trellis was sturdy. He knew it was. He'd built it himself in that long ago time.

Should he climb it? Why not? He wouldn't hurt the girl. He'd only look at her. He wanted to see how she looked asleep. She resembled Estelle so much . . .

He had one foot on the trellis when he heard it.

A frightened whimper, and then a low bark.

It was the same dog as the other night. The one that sounded like Roxie, when Roxie was afraid of something. How could he forget the sounds she'd made when he . . . ? But no, this dog couldn't possibly be Roxie. Roxie was . . . with the others.

He stepped down from the trellis and peered around in the dark.

Nothing. There was nothing here.

And yet that dog sounded so close.

The dog whimpered again. And then barked. Louder this time. Louder and yet hollow, somehow, almost like an echo. Not quite right.

He felt the hairs on his arms rise. A feeling of danger.

Where was that dog? Maybe he should leave. The dog might rouse the family.

He hurried down the lawn toward the deep woods that looked like a huge black void in the moonlight. He kept glancing back anxiously over his shoulder. If the dog decided to chase him, he would make a run for it and lose himself in the woods.

No. No movement from the deck. Nothing coming toward him. Maybe the dog had gone away, or back to sleep.

And then he was at the oak tree and the fishpond with its broken stones, and he slipped quietly into the safety of the dark pine woods.

The low, hollow bark of the dog awakened Kathy. She moaned a little, turning over and pulling her blankets up about her ears.

She wasn't getting into all that again tonight. The dog. The landing.

Especially the landing.

The landing didn't frighten her anymore. Well, not really. True, she always felt a chill there, but it wasn't that deep, unnatural cold she'd felt the day they moved in, and the night when she'd thought that a dog . . .

Dog. Mitzi. Why did Mitzi refuse to cross the landing? She'd sit on the top step, staring wistfully at Kathy's room, but if you tried to drag her out on the landing she'd go nutsy-dog, yelping and rolling her eyes. Kathy always had to carry her in her arms to her room. Dumb dog.

And the sensation of someone *listening*? No. Not since that terrible night. And she hadn't heard that strange, hissing silence again, either.

And yet, why did it always seem quieter, more silent on the landing than it did anywhere else in the house?

She moved her head restlessly on the pillow, searching for a more comfortable spot.

And that dog out back. Where did it come from?

It sounded like the one she'd heard the other night. Maybe it belonged to a neighbor.

That neighbor really ought to take better care of his dog.

The dog sounded lost. Frightened. Poor thing!

11

Matt was definitely interested in her.
Personally. Romantically. Kathy was sure of it
now.

It had started right away. After that first
lunch together.

At first she'd thought he was singling her
out simply because she'd come up with some
ideas for a couple of new columns for the
Brentwood Bugle. But even she had to admit
they really weren't *that* good. Not good enough
to explain the way he'd looked at her as he
walked her to fifth-period class that day.

"I bet you're a good dancer," he'd said. "I can
tell by the way you walk."

And then he'd been watching for her at
homeroom the next day, smiling at her over the
heads of the other kids, beckoning her to a seat
beside him. And he'd waited for her outside the
biology lab at lunch time, so he could walk her to
the cafeteria.

He'd made sure he sat next to her at the

newspaper staff's regular table, too. That day and the next.

And then, the following day, when Hank Irving started to sit down in Matt's chair, Matt had warned him away with *that look*, and she'd seen everyone exchange glances, raise their eyebrows and smile.

And that was it. She was Matt's girl. She hadn't guessed it could be so quick and so simple.

She still wasn't used to being paired with Matt that way, though. It didn't seem quite real. It was almost too wonderful. He was gorgeous. He was smart. He was . . . everything.

"So you and Matt are dating now," Beth said when Kathy called her with the latest update. "But is it *heavy* dating?"

"What do you mean—heavy dating?"

"I mean, like, do you both think that this is IT?"

"Really, Beth," Kathy had protested lamely, blushing. "We're only sixteen!"

"Romeo and Juliet were younger than that, and they knew it was true love," Beth said dreamily.

"Yeah, sure. True love, a quickie marriage, and a double suicide," Kathy retorted. "No, Beth, Matt and I are more like into dates at Kilroy's Hamburger Haven, and the Pizza Shack."

"Okay, Kathy. But my incredible powers of ESP tell me this is the start of something big. Trust me."

For all her cool, blonde good looks, Kathy actually hadn't had much experience with boys. She'd always been a little shy around them. A little unsure about what to say to a guy when they were alone on a date. Some guys misread that for aloofness. Last year, the quarterback for the school team had started referring to her as "the ice princess," but her friends had put a quick stop to that.

But she was different with Matt.

It was easy to talk to him because the two of them had a lot in common. She'd found that out right away.

For one thing, they were both bookworms. That was her word for it. "Inveterate readers," was Matt's. She'd had to look the word up in her dictionary.

"What *inveterate reader* means, basically, is *bookworm*," she told him afterward. "So why didn't you just say *bookworm*?"

"Because I wanted to impress you," Matt said. "I wanted you to know that I'm not just another pretty face."

And they both had dreams of becoming successful writers someday. Matt wanted to be an investigative reporter and win a Pulitzer Prize. Kathy wanted to write the Great American Novel.

"There, see?" Matt had accused. "I knew that very first day when you came sashaying down the aisle at homeroom that you were a writer."

"Sashay? And what, precisely, do you mean by that, Mr. Hamilton?"

"Look it up in your beloved *Funk and Wagnall's*," Matt replied with a cheeky grin. "That's how one learns, my dear Miss Colby."

Kathy was surprised that she'd told Matt

about wanting to become a writer. That was something she hadn't told anyone. Not even Beth. But that's how it was with her and Matt. It seemed they could discuss just about anything.

So it was inevitable that she would ask him what he knew about her house.

It was Friday, the day after Timothy had come home with his question about their house being "bad." Kathy had been thinking about it all day.

The office of the *Brentwood Bugle* was empty. It usually was on Friday afternoons. Everyone had rushed home to get ready for the weekend.

Everyone but Kathy and Matt. They'd been stuck with office cleanup.

"Whew, what slobs," Matt said, sweeping up the last bits of litter and throwing them into the trash can. "Ready to lock up now, Kathy?"

"In a minute," Kathy said. "But first, there's something I need to ask you."

Matt perched on one of the work tables and drew his legs up yoga style. "Sure. Shoot."

"You've lived in Brentwood all your life, haven't you?"

"Yes, I'm one of the honored few around here that have. Why?"

"Then you must know about my house. What happened in it, I mean."

Matt didn't reply.

"You do know about my house, don't you?"

"Yes. I recognized it the first time I drove you home."

Kathy glared at him accusingly. "So why didn't you ever say anything?"

Matt shrugged. "I hoped you didn't know. And I figured that, even if you did, there was no reason to bring up the unpleasant past."

"Can you tell me what happened?" Kathy asked. "About the murders?"

Matt looked at her quizzically. "You know," he said, "if you're that interested, you could probably look the story up in the newspapers. The library has all the old issues."

"I wanted to," Kathy admitted, "but Mom said I shouldn't. She made me promise. So all I know is what the real estate agent told my folks when she sold them the house. You know, that ten years ago a previous owner went crazy and killed his family. I'd like to know the entire story, though."

"Any particular reason?" Matt asked.

"Yes. One of the kids in Timmy's class told him the house was 'bad.' I thought that maybe, if I knew the facts, I could answer any questions he might have later on."

And maybe this will answer some of my questions, too. Like, what happened on that landing?

"Well, okay, if you insist. I was only six at the time, but I know most of the details. My uncle was one of the investigators for the state police. They were called in because the case was too big for the local authorities to handle. My family talked about it for years—whenever they thought we kids weren't listening, of course."

"I do know the man's name. Charles Winston," Kathy volunteered.

"That's right," said Matt. "This Charles Winston was a state department official whose star was rising. He had it all, Kathy. An education at all the right schools, a beautiful wife, and three smart, good-looking kids. As if that wasn't enough, he'd had a couple of really prestigious overseas tours of duty in the right places and in the right jobs that pretty much cinched his future promotions."

"He must have been smart, then," Kathy said slowly. "And fairly stable, emotionally."

"Well, he was, according to all his friends and co-workers. And what's really weird was that, just before the murders, everybody thought he was a real hero."

"What do you mean?"

"He'd been wounded in a bomb attack on a marketplace somewhere in the Mideast. He'd flung himself in front of some children and saved their lives. I think that was the story. Anyway, he got pretty torn up by the bomb and had been sent home for a couple months of convalescent leave before reporting in to some high-powered job in Washington."

He paused and explained. "He'd bought this house some years before, because it's close to Washington. They kept it rented whenever they were overseas. As I said, he came home a hero. He got all kinds of awards and they wrote him up in newspapers all across the country."

"And this is the man who killed his wife and

children?" Kathy asked. "I don't understand it, Matt. What changed him?"

"That's what nobody could figure out. I mean, here this guy was, the perfect husband and father. But later, a couple of old friends said that, just before the murders, Winston acted a bit distant and preoccupied. And that his wife—I think her name was Esther or Estelle or something like that—seemed worried about him. But nobody took it seriously at the time. Winston was one of those quiet, brainy types that always act wise and inscrutable."

"And then he simply upped and murdered his family," Kathy said. "It's so unbelievable, Matt."

"Yes. It happened right around this time of the year, too. The Winstons' neighbors had become worried when they hadn't seen the family for a couple of days. The newspapers had started to pile up, and no one answered the door or the phone."

Matt broke off. "Are you sure you want to hear the rest of this, Kathy?"

Kathy nodded. "Yes. I've got to or I'll go crazy, imagining things."

"Well, finally, at the request of the neighbors, the police broke in." He paused for a moment. "And what they found was three corpses—Mrs. Winston and two of her three sons. A funny, foreign looking cross had been carved with a knife on each of their foreheads, almost like a ritual killing. They'd been dead for about four days."

Kathy could barely whisper. "How did he kill them, then? With the knife?"

"No. At least he spared them that. He poisoned them. In cocoa, presumably prepared by Daddy Dearest. The empty mugs were still on the kitchen table."

"But you said only two of the sons' bodies were found in the house. Where was the third one?"

"The youngest—the seven-year-old—had obviously survived the effects of the poison longer than the others. Maybe he hadn't drunk as much. I don't know. Anyway, his body was found at the far end of the garden, down by the fishpond. He was evidently running from his father. Or maybe *to* someone. Or something."

Kathy cleared her throat. "But how did the police know it was the father who did it? I mean, the story I heard was that he disappeared. Maybe he was murdered, too."

"No, the father did it, all right. His fingerprints were on the cocoa cups. And the poison was one of those things people buy to kill rodents and bugs in their gardens. He had to sign for it. They remembered him at the store, and had his signature to prove it. And the bag had been opened and used."

Maybe Mom was right, Kathy thought. *Maybe I was better off not knowing. No. Ignorance only makes fear worse. I have to know.*

"Oh," Matt said cautiously. "There was something else. He killed the family dog, too."

"A dog?" Kathy echoed faintly.

"Yes, a little black Border collie. He did it with the knife. Evidently the dog gave him quite a chase. They found its blood on the landing and on the floor and the doggie door in the kitchen. It had managed to make it outside. But Winston must have caught up with the dog on the deck, because that's where they found the body."

Kathy's head was whirling. "They . . . they found the dog's blood on the landing? Wh . . . what about the landing?"

Matt looked at her and said carefully. "I don't think I should tell you any more, Kathy. It's obviously affecting you. You're pale as a ghost."

"You've got to," Kathy said angrily. "I have to know, Matt. Don't you understand? If you don't tell me, I'll only imagine things, and that's even worse."

Matt sighed and raised his hands in a helpless gesture. "Okay. I'll tell you, then. The landing was where they found the three bodies. He'd propped them up in a row, their backs to the wall. But they found the dog outside, on the deck."

12

The upstairs landing was now a loathsome place to Kathy.

She imagined how the corpses must have looked, three of them, bloated with death and seated in a row, their backs against the wall, their eyes staring sightlessly forward.

And those eerie, foreign-looking crosses carved in blood on their pale foreheads.

Why? Why did he do it?

And what had they been thinking when they died, that woman and her children? The little one who tried to run away—he was only seven years old, poor little darling. Timothy's age. He'd been trying to run away from his own father— his murderous father—when he died. No one with him. No one to hold his hand and give him courage in his final, agonized moments.

And the dog. The dog whose death had begun on the landing and ended on the deck.

That night . . . the night I thought there was a dog on the landing. Was it . . . ?

No, of course it wasn't. It was only a sweater, a fuzzy woolen sweater I'd felt. This is why Mom didn't want me to find out more about the murders. Because I'd start seeing ghosts everywhere.

Maybe she was right. Maybe I was better off, not knowing.

Then: *No. I would have found out sooner or later. Better to know now, so I can learn to deal with it.*

"That silly little Mitzi won't go out back to do her thing," Mrs. Colby complained the next day at breakfast. "She absolutely refuses to set foot on the deck."

The deck!

"Maybe she's gotten used to the front lawn," Kathy said cautiously. *Mom must never know!* "She always goes under that bush you pointed out to her when we first got here. You know what a creature of habit Mitzi is. She just likes the front yard, that's all."

"But we have this big backyard and yet—" Mrs. Colby began.

"Mitzi's a city dog, Mom," Kathy interrupted. "She likes to see cars go by. So why not let her have her way?"

Please don't make an issue of it, Mom. You don't want to know what Mitzi sees out there on the deck.

Kathy started feeling the cold on the landing again, too.

She learned to grit her teeth and cross it as

quickly as possible. What else could she do? Who could she talk to about what was happening to her? Certainly not her parents. What she felt about the landing was a closed issue with them. And she didn't dare tell Beth. Beth was too practical, too down-to-earth to understand what was going on here.

Matt, maybe? No. They could discuss just about anything, but not this. "It's all my fault," he would say. "You're only feeling this way because I told you the story of the murders. I shouldn't have."

And then there would be an awkwardness, a constraint, between them. She didn't want that. Not with Matt.

On Sunday morning, over their usual Belgian waffle brunch, Mrs. Colby said, "It's such a nice day. Let's go to the Washington Zoo."

"Oh boy," Timothy said. "Can I see the pandas? And can I take Philip?"

Mr. and Mrs. Colby exchanged glances. The meaning was clear. Whenever Timothy insisted on bringing an imaginary friend with him, people stared and then immediately moved aside. The sight of a child talking to an invisible companion was, to put it mildly, unsettling.

"Nooo," Mrs. Colby said, with a fake, bland smile. "Let's just make it a family outing this time, darling."

"I won't be able to come," Kathy said quickly. She hated zoos. She hated the smells, especially in the monkey house. "I've got a paper to write for English Lit."

But after they'd left, Kathy began to have second thoughts. The house was quiet. Too quiet.

And later, studying in the den, she found herself moving quietly, too. Tiptoeing from couch to chair. From chair to the kitchen for a snack.

Mitzi had attached herself to Kathy like a limpet. She leaned sideways against Kathy, her silky head warm against her leg, when Kathy sat in a chair. And she followed anxiously along behind, never breaking physical contact, when Kathy got up and walked around.

"Mitzi! What is it with you?" Kathy whispered. "Are you spooking me, or am I spooking you?"

And then Kathy realized she had to go upstairs. She'd left her notes up in her room. She couldn't write her paper without them.

Should she wait and do the paper later tonight, when everyone was home, or should she go up the stairs, right this minute, and get those notes?

This was her house. She had to face her fears sooner or later.

Okay, it would be sooner. It would be now, as a matter of fact.

Mitzi accompanied her only as far as the foyer. Then the little dog sat down and refused to go a step further.

Kathy put one foot on the bottom stair and hesitated.

Behind her, Mitzi was making odd, squeaky, whimpery little noises in the back of her throat.

Kathy turned and looked at her. Mitzi's eyes were wide. Fearful.

"Okay, Mitzi," she said. "Watch me. There's absolutely nothing to be afraid of, okay?"

As she mounted the stairs, the coldness that usually lingered only on the landing swept down toward her, slowing her climb, and she found herself listening . . . listening . . . to the sound of silence.

Her ears rang.

Is this what *They*—The Listeners—hear? she asked herself. Silence? Or are they waiting for something? Or someone?

And if so, what? What is it they want?

She ran quickly up the rest of the stairs and stood in the middle of the landing, her hands balled into fists.

"Stop it!" she shouted. "Stop it! Do you hear me? I can't help you. It's too late. Go away— please go away—and leave me . . . us . . . alone!"

Nothing. Still that terrible, ringing silence.

That . . . *listening*.

She tried again.

"I'm your friend, can't you see that? No one here means you any harm. It's a different house now. We're happy here. We all love each other. It's time you found peace and rest, too. So leave this house. Go. What happened to you is . . . over!"

The cold deepened.

"Then—damn you!" she said, turning on her heel.

She started for her bedroom but found she

could not move. She strained to move forward across the landing, but something held her back. Something pleading. Anxious.

Stay. Help us.

Had she heard someone whisper that? No. There hadn't been any sound. Only that ringing silence.

She tried again to move, but it was no use. She was rooted to the spot.

"Let me go!" she shouted. "Do you hear me? I said, let me go! Leave me alone. I want nothing to do with you!"

And then, suddenly, she was released, as if the bonds that held her had been abruptly severed.

She staggered and nearly fell, but the force that formerly had restrained her now kept her from falling. Buoyed her up. Gently. Tenderly.

"Who are you?" Kathy whispered. "What do you want of me?"

No answer. But again, in that ringing silence, Kathy had the feeling that *someone was listening.*

13

Later, as Kathy sat trembling on her bed, she asked herself what she should do.

Should she tell her parents about what had just happened? That she'd stood there, listening to the silence and talking to what she thought were the ghosts of a murdered family? And that she'd slipped, but an unseen force—spectral hands, maybe—had kept her from falling?

No. Definitely no. It sounded crazy, even to her.

Mom and Dad would think she'd flipped her lid. They didn't believe in ghosts and the supernatural. As soon as they found out that Matt had told her the whole story of the murders, they would say it was just as they'd feared. Now that she'd gone and poked around and unearthed all the gory details of the murder, her imagination had run away with her.

Mom would say, "Didn't I warn you not to do that, Kathy?"

Or worse could happen. They might send her

to a psychiatrist. Her and Timothy. One had imaginary friends. The other had imaginary ghosts.

And what would her new friends think about her, then?

What would Matt think?

Or, worse than worse, maybe her parents would be angry at Matt for telling her about the murders, and forbid her to see him again.

No, she thought. I'd better keep my mouth shut.

Her mother's words came to her—that they should forget what had taken place in this house. That, after all, a house is only plaster and wood, and that it is happy or unhappy depending on the people living in it.

But out there, on the landing . . .

No. It will go away. It has to go away.

She remembered reading that sometimes, when people died violent deaths, a remnant of their energy force field was left behind, like an echo of the last, fading notes of a song.

She felt better, calmer, when she thought of her experience out there as something that could be explained by science. An echo? Yes, she could understand that.

And the force—hands?—that had first restrained her and then kept her from falling, was it . . . *they* . . . a part of the echo, too? Or could it have been something caused by the terror of the moment? That she'd been too frightened to move? That did happen to people, and she'd almost been out of her head there, for a minute, hadn't she?

And would it happen again, the listening?

No. Echoes do die, don't they? So these will die, too. They have to die. We're filling the house with a new kind of energy that will erase the past, the echoes.

Yes, but maybe she was keeping the echoes alive with her thoughts of the murder. What if she was the one who was holding them here?

Then she must forget about the house's terrible past. Put it out of her mind entirely. Channel her thoughts elsewhere on positive, happy things.

Yes, we will make it a happy house. And I will begin, right now, by forgetting everything I have heard about the Winston murders.

I will forget. I *will* forget.

Two days later, after school, someone rang the doorbell.

Mrs. Colby answered and Kathy watched from the hall.

Her mother recoiled when she saw a heavily bearded, rather dirty and disreputable looking man.

She half closed the door, jamming her foot against it, so he couldn't force his way in.

He laughed, revealing a large gap of missing front teeth and said, "Oh, don't worry, lady. I won't hurt you. I'm Dennis. Everyone knows me. I do odd jobs around the neighborhood."

His voice was surprisingly cultivated, at odds with his appearance.

Mrs. Colby relaxed a little. "Odd jobs?" she asked. "Like what?"

"Oh, gardening. Carpentry. Things like that," Dennis replied with an airy wave. "I can give you references. The lady next door—Mrs. Lilley—I've done quite a bit of work for her."

"You do gardening?" Mrs. Colby asked hopefully.

"Yes, indeed. Just ask Mrs. Farnsworth, across the street," Dennis said. "I do all her mowing and trimming."

"Well," Mrs. Colby said thoughtfully. "We *do* need a lot done to the backyard. Weeding. Mulching. That sort of thing."

"Yes," Dennis said. "I've noticed. This house has been kept rented. You can always tell. Renters never do much gardening. They're afraid they'll move before the seeds sprout, I guess."

He laughed. Phlegm rattled in his chest. Even from where she stood, Kathy could smell his breath. Sour. Rank. She wondered when he'd last seen a dentist. Or brushed his teeth.

"Well, thank you, Mr. . . . ah, Dennis," Mrs. Colby said. "I'd like to think about your offer. I'll have to speak to my husband about it first, though."

Dennis bowed slightly. "I'll be back the day after tomorrow. I've promised to clean the storm drains for Mrs. Lilley. I'll check with you then."

"Please do," Mrs. Colby said with a smile. "I'm sure we'll have some work for you."

As soon as she'd closed the door, she rushed to the phone.

"I'm calling Mrs. Lilley," she told Kathy, punching buttons, the phone to her ear. "I'm sure he's telling the truth, but you can never be too careful."

"Oh, Mrs. Lilley?" she said into the phone. "This rather strange-looking man just came by. He says he does odd jobs. Gardening. Yard work. And . . . Yes, Dennis. That was the name he gave me. Right. Bad teeth. Big, dirty beard. Okay, I thought I'd better check. He's trustworthy, you say? Good. I can certainly use someone around the yard. Great."

Her voice changed. Softened. Became more charming. Her social voice, Kathy thought.

"Oh, thank you," Mrs. Colby said. "Yes, we'd love to meet the rest of the neighborhood. How thoughtful of you. Friday? We'd be delighted to come. Can I bring anything? Are you sure? Thank you. We'll look forward to coming."

She hung up the phone.

"Well, Kathy," Mrs. Colby said, beaming. "It seems we've found our gardener. And we've been invited to Mrs. Lilley's to meet our neighbors. Things are certainly looking up, aren't they?"

14

Why have these people usurped my house?
the man asked himself.

Were they mocking him?

First he'd seen Philip playing in the tree
house. Philip who shouldn't be here any more,
who was supposed to be with the others. And
then the girl. The one with the same haunting,
silver-pale hair as Philip and Estelle.

Was she trying to look like Estelle? Was she
toying with him, in an attempt to confuse him? Is
that what she was doing?

He'd come by the house, pretending to look
for work. A clever ruse, he'd thought. Actually, of
course, he'd really come to see Philip. To see if
Philip was still living in the house.

Philip wasn't there, but the girl was. She'd
stood in the shadows of the front hall, watching
him. What had she been thinking?

The house, what he could see of it, looked
well set up. Good quality furniture. Expensive
drapes at the windows. And then the talk of

needing someone to fix up the back garden. It sounded as if they intended to stay.

So what should he do now? This house was supposed to be kept empty, sacred to the memory of those who had given their last full measure to The Cause.

But They—The Voices—hadn't contacted him lately. He wanted to do Their will. They knew that. And yet They only came to him briefly now, parceling out Their instructions a little at a time.

Why did They keep him waiting and on edge like this? Was endless patience yet another sacrifice They were asking of him? How many more sacrifices would They require before Their promises to him were fulfilled?

It's been so long already, he thought sadly. *Haven't I waited ten years for Them to bring Their vision to glorious reality?*

They said They would make the world a paradise if he did what They asked.

And he had.

The sacrifice. The ultimate sacrifice.

What Abraham, in the Bible, had been prepared to do to Isaac.

He remembered how it had all started. That bomb in the Middle Eastern marketplace. He'd been injured. A head injury. There was something wrong with his head. He could scarcely think for the red haze of pain that fastened, like a vise, around his skull, squeezing it tighter and tighter.

But he could hear. He could hear, all around him, the terrible screaming and moaning of the wounded.

The babies. The sound of the babies shrieking. That was the worst part. It made the pain worse. Made it knife through his very brain until . . .

Until he saw the white light. The white light that took away the pain and the sounds of death.

And then he heard a gentle murmuring of voices. Soft, at first, and distant. Then growing louder. Coming closer.

The white light grew brighter and brighter, and he could hear, now, what they were saying:

"Do as we command, and mankind shall be returned to what it was, in the beginning, before the Fall of Adam. The Lion shall lie down with the Lamb if you do as we say . . . "

And now . . . what? Was he being tested yet again? Yes, that must be it. He was being tested.

15

"**Dennis is working out quite well,**" Mrs. Colby reported happily the next afternoon. "He put in his first morning's work today. He made a great deal of headway in the back garden."

"I didn't think he was supposed to come back for a couple of days," Kathy said, laying her books down on the kitchen table and opening the refrigerator. "Is there any fruit juice left, Mom?"

"Behind the milk, I think," Mrs. Colby replied. "I was lucky. Dennis simply appeared at the door this morning and said he had a cancellation. So he started right in. You can see a difference out there already. He's coming again tomorrow morning to finish the weeding. And then, when his schedule allows, he'll be back to trim and mulch around the bushes."

Kathy poured herself a glass of apple juice and took a cookie from the jar.

"I wish you hadn't hired him, Mom."

Her mother raised her eyebrows. "Why?"

"I don't know. He scares me. He acts so

creepy or something. And he looks like a were-wolf with that dirty old beard of his."

"Really, Kathy, he's very trustworthy," Mrs. Colby said. "He does odd jobs for just about every family in this neighborhood. And Ellen Lilley recommends him highly."

"How long has he been working for her?"

"Oh, I don't know. A month or so, I think."

"Does she know anything about him?" Kathy persisted, finishing her juice and placing the glass in the sink. "Like, where he lives and whether he has a family?"

"She said he has no family. And that he lives in an old, broken-down trailer at the edge of town. The trailer park is pretty terrible looking, but she says he's trying to save up enough money to go back to California. He hates the cold."

"Well, promise me you won't let him into the house, Mom, when you're here alone."

Her mother laughed. "I can't promise you that. If no one else around here thinks he's dangerous, why should I?"

Kathy shrugged. "Well, okay, if you're sure. But he still looks creepy to me."

And then she turned and whistled for Mitzi.

Mitzi didn't like being carried across the landing any more than Kathy liked crossing it.

But Kathy needed to get to her room, and even Mitzi's wriggling, protesting body was company, and better than going it alone.

"Philip gave me a picture of himself today," Timothy said at supper.

He looked around, startled by the immediate, riveted attention his announcement received.

"Well, he did," he said defensively. "I'm not making it up!"

Mr. Colby, who'd frozen in the act of scooping a helping of mashed potatoes onto his plate, now carefully laid the spoon back in the bowl.

"A picture? Of Philip?" he asked. "What kind of picture?"

"You mean, you *drew* a picture of Philip. That's what you're saying, isn't it, darling?" asked Mrs. Colby, leaning forward anxiously.

"No, a picture. A real picture. Like what you take with a camera," Timothy insisted.

"Could we see it?" Kathy asked. *Now what far out story was Timmy coming up with to explain his imaginary friends?*

"Yeah, sure," Timmy said. He had to half stand, pushing the chair back noisily, to pull the photo from a back pocket. "Here."

He held it up so all could see—a grubby, worn photo of a small, pale boy with silvery-blonde hair, blowing out the candles of a birthday cake.

So Philip was real after all!

And Timothy was right. Philip *did* look like him.

"There's something written on the back, too," Timmy told them. "Philip says his mother wrote it."

Mrs. Colby took the picture and studied the writing.

"Philip, on his seventh birthday," she read.

"His mother has lovely handwriting, Timmy. Very graceful."

"Philip says he loves his mother. She's real pretty, he says."

Mrs. Colby passed the photo to her husband. "There's something else written on the back, Jim, but I can't make it out."

Mr. Colby reached in his pocket and pulled out his reading glasses.

"I can't read it either," he said after studying it carefully. "It's a date, maybe, but it's illegible."

Kathy got up from her chair and stood behind her father, leaning over his shoulder for a closer look at the photo.

"That picture looks like it's been through a couple of wars," she said.

"It does look pretty beat-up," agreed Mr. Colby, fingering a worn, discolored edge.

"Well, I like it," Timmy said loudly. "Philip gave it to me, and he's my friend. It was on the wall of the tree house. He said he knew it was kind of dirty, but he liked it anyway."

"Really, darling, we didn't mean to criticize," murmured Mrs. Colby.

"Philip says his birthday was a real happy day," Timmy went on. "They had this big party for him and everyone brought presents. He says I can have the picture because I'm his very best friend."

Mr. and Mrs. Colby exchanged joyful glances.

"To tell you the truth, Timothy," Mrs. Colby said hesitantly, "we thought maybe Philip was another one of your imaginary friends. We're so happy to find out he's real, and that the two of you get along so well."

"I don't have imaginary friends any more, Mom," he said scornfully. "That's baby stuff. Philip and I are big guys."

Mom, not Mommy, Kathy thought. *Maybe Timmy really is growing up at long last!*

Aloud she said, "I'd like to meet Philip some time. Why don't you bring him to the house?"

Timmy shook his head. "Philip doesn't like my house. He says it's a bad house. It scares him."

"Oh dear." Mrs. Colby sighed. "I guess that nasty little Brian at school has been frightening Philip, too. But we know better, don't we, Timmy? Remember our little talk?"

Timmy just set his jaw stubbornly. "If Philip doesn't want to come to my house, he doesn't have to."

"Well, okay," Kathy said. "But I'd still like to meet him. Maybe I'll come down to the tree house tomorrow."

"No," Timmy said firmly. "Girls aren't allowed in our tree house."

"Does that mean I'll never meet Philip, then?" Kathy asked.

"But you have," Timothy said. "Philip says you've walked right past him a couple of times and you haven't even noticed him."

Kathy laughed. "Well, I won't next time, Timmy. I'll be watching for him. And please tell him to speak up and let me know he's there."

That night, Kathy dreamed she heard whispers on the landing.

Soft whispers. Whispers of entreaty.

Or were they warning her of something? Some impending danger?

But with the diamond-bright November sunlight streaming through her window the next morning, it was hard to remember the whispers of the night.

16

"I love you madly, Kathy Colby."

Yes, that's what Matt said. And in front of everyone.

He'd said it jokingly, of course, but the words were still there. And he'd given her that special smile.

It happened at the first meeting of the planning committee for the annual Christmas dance. They'd added their names to the sign-up list because, as Matt had said with mock seriousness, "A reporter has to be *everywhere*!"

"Okay, you guys," Kim Warren, the committee head said, banging on the desk with her palms to call the group to order. "They've given this dance to our class this year. This is our big chance to show up the Seniors. We've got to think of a really good theme. One that hasn't been worked to death. So how about it —any ideas?"

"What about *The Night Before Christmas*?" suggested Mimi Ammenhauser timidly. Mimi was a small, thin girl who got straight A's. "Everybody could come like something out of the poem."

"Forget it, Mimi," said Lefty Levine. "I'm not coming dressed like a sugarplum."

"And reindeer costumes are kind of hard to find this time of year," snickered Artie Van Dorn.

"*Snowflake Ball* might be a good theme," said Sallie Johnson. "We could decorate the gym with these huge, glittery snowflakes and—"

"They did that three years ago," Kim said. She consulted her notes. "And they've used the *Sleigh Ride* theme before, too. And *A Visit to the North Pole* with the entire cheerleading team as elves in tights and minis."

"Darn, where was I that year?" Lefty Levine said, smacking his brow.

"What did they do last year?" Kathy asked.

"That was the best ever," answered Mimi dreamily, flipping back her long red hair. "They called it, *The Twelve Days of Christmas*. And they simply went mad with *papier mâché*." She gave the words their full French pronunciation. "The chairperson that year was a senior and had an art scholarship to—"

"Well, I'm not in favor of doing anything like that," Sallie snapped. "It's too much work."

"You want something radical and different?" Matt asked, looking around. "I'll give you radical. Let's have a plain old dance. Girls in formals. Guys in tuxes. Balloons and streamers. That sort of thing."

"Really, Matt," Kim said, raising her eyebrows.

"How common! That would make us a laughing-stock. Our class reputation rides on this dance."

Artie rolled his eyes at Lefty. He spoke in a falsetto, raising his eyebrows in an imitation of Kim. "Yes, Matthew. Your common, peasant blood is showing again. Formals and tuxes—how vulgar!"

"Yeah," said Lefty. "Everyone knows the girls would have fits if they couldn't wear fancy costumes to this thing."

"Wait a minute!" Mimi cried, raising her hand for silence. "I've got it!"

Kim pounded the desk again. "Everybody listen up."

"How about . . ." Mimi's eyes glowed . . . "A Dickensian Christmas!"

"A *what?*" asked Lefty.

"Like in Dickens' *Christmas Carol*," Mimi went on. "We could decorate the gym like a London street, and we could all wear period costumes and—"

Someone made a rude noise.

"Are you nuts, Mimi?" cried Artie. "Where would we get all the decorations? Or period costumes? Not that we would need them, because nobody would come, anyway. Jeez, Mimi. *Dickens!*"

Kathy cleared her throat and spoke up. "Mimi might have an idea there."

Matt looked at her in disbelief, as did everyone else.

"No, listen," said Kathy. "I don't mean a Christmas out of Dickens, but remember in *A*

Christmas Carol when the Ghost of Christmas Future appeared?"

There were a few nods.

"Well, we could have a Christmas Future dance. A Space Age Christmas, don't you see?" She began to talk faster as she warmed to the idea. "We can all come like people from the future—the way they'd dress for a Christmas dance."

She looked around her. The others were sitting up, listening. "Costumes would be easy to do. The more far-out the better. Lots of aluminum foil and wires. Or even tights and tunics, like in *Star Trek*. And decorations would be easy, too. We'd need some strobe lights and blow-up posters of the moon walk and shuttle lift-offs. That sort of thing. Maybe we could get the stage crew to help us build a rocket ship out of plywood and spray paint it silver and—"

"And a huge, glittery Twenty-first Century Christmas tree," said Kim. "Really spacy looking! I can see it now."

"Neat idea, Kathy," said Artie.

They were all staring at her approvingly. She knew, then, that she'd finally been accepted, really accepted, by the kids at Brentwood High.

And that's when Matt had said, "Kathy, you're something else! No wonder I love you madly!"

Afterward, when they were alone, Matt said, "I wasn't kidding, Kathy. I really meant what I said about you being special. I knew it the minute you walked into homeroom that day."

He put his arms around her and drew her to him. She could smell his clean, fresh scent.

"I wish there was something I could give you," he said. "To wear, I mean. Like my class ring— only we haven't gotten them yet. Something that would say 'hands off' to the other guys."

Kathy smiled. "I think you just did. Back there, in front of the planning committee. Besides, my class ring will be just like yours."

"But mine's bigger," he said. "More gold. You could wear mine around your neck on a chain. And I could wear yours on my pinkie finger."

Kathy's smile widened. She knew she probably looked goofy, but she didn't care.

She was happy. Really, truly happy.

And she wasn't going to allow anything to spoil it.

Not even . . . ?

No. Not even *that*.

17

Matt drove Kathy home that afternoon.
He'd talked his older brother into selling him—
on the installment plan, of course—his old grey
Plymouth Duster. And now he and Kathy drove
to and from school together every day.

"Can you come in, Matt?" Kathy asked as
she gathered up her books.

"Thanks, but not this afternoon. I promised
Mom I'd help her clean out the attic. I'll call you
later, though."

Kathy waved as he pulled away. And then
she saw Dennis, the handyman, raking leaves in
the yard across the street.

That man really *is* scary looking, she
thought, turning away quickly and hurrying up
the path to the front door.

*I must be more careful, the man told himself.
That girl, the one with the pale hair, is no fool.
I've seen the expression on her face when she
looks at me. She suspects something, I can tell.*

He gathered up the last of the leaves, thrust them into the trash bag and carried it down to the curb. There, done for the day. He didn't really like doing yard work. Hated it, actually. But how else could he loiter around the old neighborhood without attracting attention?

That girl, though ... she was trouble. He had a strong feeling about that. He'd better watch out for her. She puzzled him. The way she made herself look like Estelle. Was it just a coincidence she looked like that or was she doing it to torment him?

No. He mustn't worry. His way would be made smooth. They—The Voices that came with the bright, white light—would take care of everything. He had to have faith, They told him. Hadn't They guided his footsteps all these years?

He remembered with satisfaction how he'd gotten away that November day, ten years ago.

He'd driven west to the Blue Ridge mountains, to a remote area he'd discovered once on a solitary camping trip. He had provisions in the car, and clothes—the oldest, scruffiest-looking ones he could find at the Salvation Army store in Washington. And he had enough money to tide him over for a long, long time in the money belt he wore around his waist.

Oh, he'd had a good laugh, holed up in his hidden cave, eating Spam, while he knew dozens of FBI agents were frantically searching for him at airports and train stations. Naturally they'd figured he'd try to leave the country, but he'd

fooled them again, hadn't he? They—The Voices—
had told him what to do, and They were always
right.

It hadn't taken long for his hair and beard to
grow out. He let them alone, not washing or
combing them, and they were shaggy and dirty
looking. And he'd thrown away the toupee that
covered that bald spot on top. It was his little
secret. His and Estelle's. Going without it really
altered his appearance. Made him look years
older.

He'd thrown away his false tooth, too. The
one in the front. Estelle would have a fit, he
thought, if she could see me now!

Then he'd thought, no, wait a minute. Estelle
was gone. Forever.

It was hard, what he had done to her and the
boys but, after all, he was a prophet, a savior,
wasn't he, come to rescue mankind? The Voices
had warned him it wouldn't be easy.

Finally They told him it was time to leave
the mountains. He'd pushed his old green station
wagon, long before, over the cliff into the waters
of an old, deserted quarry, so he'd had to walk to
the nearest town and get on a bus for New York
City. That was where They told him to go.

Again he had to marvel at Their—the Voices—
wisdom.

It was easy to get lost in New York City.
Especially when you were a street person. No one pays
much attention to you when you're a street person.

Their plan was faultless. The FBI had his picture in every post office across the country and

there he was, right in the heart of New York City, and people wouldn't look him in the eye, even when he tapped them on the shoulder and asked them for money. He didn't need it really. The money. He just did it for fun. To prove he was invisible.

He figured it wouldn't be long before the world would change as the result of his sacrifice. Yet, and this disturbed him, there were still wars and rumors of wars and famines and earthquakes while, down in the streets, people were still killing each other.

In fact, all around him people were mugging and knifing and shooting each other. Yet he was safe. No one had ever harmed him.

Didn't that prove that he was protected? Invincible?

Or he would be, at least, until his mission was fulfilled. Until everyone lived in loving harmony and peace, and the Lion lay down, at last, with the Lamb.

When that happened, it didn't matter what became of him. His reward, his paradise, would be in knowing that he had brought about the return of the Garden of Eden. That, in spite of millenniums of suffering, he had returned mankind to its glorious state of innocence.

He hadn't questioned The Voices. He knew everything he'd worked and sacrificed for must happen in its own time. And yet years—ten endless years—had gone by and still the world was in darkness.

Had he done something wrong?

And then They had spoken: "Go home," They

said. "You have left something undone. Something that is impeding Our Plan."

He'd bought a van. A beat-up, outdated one, and returned to Brentwood. They had guided him once again. They led him to a trailer park on the edge of town. He could live there, undetected, and drive in daily to watch over his home.

Working in his old neighborhood as a handyman was his idea, actually. It gave him something to do and a good "cover" for his surveillance activities.

A few of his old neighbors still lived in the neighborhood and it amused him to see that they didn't recognize him. His appearance had been completely altered by the beard, the bald patch, the long, shaggy hair and the missing tooth. No—make that missing teeth. He'd lost a few more in New York. He'd dared not visit a dentist and so they'd rotted and fallen out.

And now, although he was still by rights a middle-aged man, he looked far older. Far older than his real age.

Sleeping on the streets of New York will do it to you every time, he told himself with a chuckle.

A month had passed since his return to Brentwood, and he'd been waiting to hear what it was that he had left undone.

And now he knew.

Philip had not been sacrificed with the others. He was still here.

The ultimate perfection of what he'd been asked to do was still incomplete.

Philip must die. And soon.

18

Timothy was crying when he came into the kitchen at supper time.

"Philip says he can't play with me anymore because he's going away," he sobbed.

Kathy looked up from the tomato she was slicing. "What do you mean? Where's he going?"

Timmy sat down at the table and laid his head on his arms. "I don't know. Far away, I think." His voice was muffled.

Mrs. Colby went over to him and sat beside him, patting his back. "Maybe he's just going on a little trip, darling. A nice trip with his parents. And then he'll be back."

"No. It isn't a fun trip. It's not like that, Mom."

"What do you mean?"

"I mean it's bad. Real bad."

Mrs. Colby took Timmy by the shoulders and raised him to an upright position. "Listen, Timmy, you are going to have to tell me what Philip said. But first, wipe your nose."

She handed him a tissue. "There, that's better. Now. Start from the beginning."

Timmy took a deep breath. "I waited and waited and finally Philip came to the tree house. But he said he couldn't play because he was going away. And then he left."

"Did he say why he had to go away?" Kathy asked, laying down her paring knife and joining them at the table.

"Yes. It's his father. He says his father is going to hurt him."

"Hurt him?" Kathy echoed.

"Yeah. Like he hurt his brothers, he said." Timmy's eyes were wide and frightened. "Philip is really scared of his father."

"Wh . . . what happened to his brothers?" Kathy asked faintly.

"I don't know," said Timmy, "but Philip says he hurt them bad."

"Oh dear God," Mrs. Colby said, pressing her hand to her mouth.

"His father's been away," Timmy continued, "but now he's back and Philip says his father will find him and hurt him. So he's got to hide from him."

"What about his mother?" Kathy asked. "Can't she do anything?"

Timmy shook his head. "No. His mother's not here."

"Where is she?"

"I don't know. Philip says she left right after his birthday."

"Where are his brothers?"

"They're gone, too. They went with his mother."

"Then who does he live with? His grandparents?" asked Mrs. Colby.

Timothy raised his small shoulders in a gesture of bewilderment. "I don't know. I don't think so, though. He never talks about them."

"Where does he live?" asked Kathy.

"I don't know that, either," Timothy replied. "He just comes to the tree house, that's all."

Mrs. Colby turned to Kathy, a stricken expression on her face. "Honestly, Kathy, I had no idea the child was so . . . alone. I can only blame myself. I should have asked Timmy about Philip days ago. Maybe I could have done something."

Kathy reached out and touched her mother's hand. It was cold and trembling. "Don't blame yourself, Mom. You didn't know. And you've been so busy unpacking and setting up the house that—"

"That I've been too busy to look right under my nose." Mrs. Colby's eyes filled with tears. "Philip is only seven years old, Kathy. Just a baby. And apparently he isn't living with members of his family, or surely he would have mentioned it to Timothy. His mother is gone, he says. And his brothers."

"I can't imagine them running off and leaving a seven-year-old—unless they feared for their lives," Kathy said. "And even then, why would they leave Philip behind? His father must be an animal."

"That's what it sounds like," said Mrs. Colby,

shuddering. "These things happen. You read about them all the time, but I never thought that . . . And now Philip is running away to save himself from a violently abusive father."

She turned to Timothy. "Did he say what he was afraid his father would do to him?"

"No," said Timmy. "But he was really scared, Mom."

Mrs. Colby wrung her hands. "If only he'd told us. If only he'd come to us with his problems. We would have taken him in and protected him."

"I told him that," Timmy said. "But Philip said no. That this was a bad house and he was scared to come here."

"Oh dear God, what will happen to him now?" Mrs. Colby said. "Alone out there somewhere." She looked out the window. "And it's getting dark, too."

"Wait a minute," Kathy said. "Maybe we can find him. What's Philip's last name, Timmy?"

"I don't know, Kathy. He never told me."

"Your teacher should certainly know, though, shouldn't she? And she's bound to have his address."

"Philip isn't in my class," Timothy said. "I don't even know if he goes to my school."

"But there are two second grades at Jefferson Elementary, right? Maybe he's in the other one."

Timmy shook his head doubtfully. "I don't think so. I've never seen Philip at school."

"Don't you ever talk about school up there in your playhouse?" Kathy asked.

"No. Philip says he doesn't like to talk about school. We pretend we're action heroes. You know, like we're big and strong and do good things to save people. And the tree house is our secret clubhouse."

"Philip must go to Timmy's school," Mrs. Colby said. "It's the one for this area."

She jumped to her feet and ran over to the wall phone. She rummaged around in a drawer of the cabinet and pulled out a list of telephone numbers. "His principal might recognize my description of Philip, even though I don't have his last name. And if there's a possibility that Philip is registered at the school, considering the emergency situation we have here, surely Mr. Besset will open up his office tonight and find Philip's records. It will help the police in their search."

"Don't forget to tell him we have a photo of Philip," Kathy said. "We can drive over to Mr. Besset's house with it. Philip might use a different first name at school."

Philip's description rang no bells with Mr. Besset.

"The only boy that age I can think of at Jefferson Elementary answering that description is your son, Mrs. Colby," he said. "But I'll have to check the records. Could you meet me at the school in ten minutes with your photo? And have you called the police?"

"No, not yet," said Mrs. Colby. "I wanted to talk to you first."

"Why don't you call them right away and explain the situation as you have explained it to me. Then ask them to meet us at the school. They will want Philip's records, if we have them, for their investigation."

"Right. Thank you, Mr. Besset."

Mrs. Colby hung up the phone and stood motionless, chewing on her bottom lip. Finally she said, "I'm sorry I have to ask you this, Timmy, but I must because the police will. Do you think there's a chance, even the tiniest, smallest chance, that Philip is . . . making this up? About his father and his running away, I mean?"

Timmy answered immediately. "No, Mom. Philip doesn't lie. And he cried when he told me about his father."

"That's good enough for me, then," said Mrs. Colby, picking up the phone again. "Write a note to Dad, Kathy, telling him where we are. Timmy, get your coat and find my car keys. We're all going over to the school."

"Philip was not registered at the school. Mr. Besset and the police went through all the records of children Philip's age. They examined the records of children in the first and third grades, too, just in case he was either ahead of or behind other children his age.

No Philip.

"So what do we do now?" Mrs. Colby asked. She, Kathy, and Timmy had waited outside in the hall while the record search was in progress.

"The child is out there somewhere. How do you propose to find him?"

"We'll put out an alert on the boy," said the senior police officer, Sergeant Martin. "With your permission, we'll keep the photo and have copies made of it. And some of our men will search the woods behind your house for him. It's the logical place for him to hide out."

"Could we help, Officer?" Kathy asked.

"Thank you, Miss, but there's no need. We know those woods. They cover only a small area. A few of our men and some dogs should be able to find just about anything hiding there."

"And if Philip isn't there?" asked Mrs. Colby. "What then?"

"We might get a missing person inquiry tonight from the people he lives with. It's still early. If not, we'll go to all the local schools tomorrow. He ought to be registered at one of them. And once we get his name and his address, we'll check out the people he lives with, as well as his neighbors. We'll try to locate his mother, too. And that father."

Sergeant Martin's eyes narrowed. "You said the boy told your son his father has 'been away.' Maybe he's been confined somewhere. If only I had his last name . . . But we can run what facts we have through the computer. Maybe we'll come up with something."

"It sounds as if you're doing all you can," Mrs. Colby said.

"Not knowing who he is makes it harder," Sergeant Martin said. "Usually the search is launched by family members and we have a lot more to go on."

"If . . . no, *when* you find Philip," Mrs. Colby said from between stiff lips, "and if he has no family willing to care for him, we would be very glad to take responsibility for him."

"That's very kind of you, Mrs. Colby," Officer Martin said. "I'm sure we'll find him. Everything will turn out okay. Don't you worry."

It was nearly midnight when Kathy finally got to bed. Her mother and father were still down in the den, talking about Philip and what they would do when he was found.

She was just falling asleep when she became aware of a change of temperature in the room. The bone-chilling cold she had felt on the landing those few, terrifying times, had now invaded her bedroom.

She tried to rise, but found she could not. Something was pressing against her. Holding her there. Not hands. Nothing she could identify. And yet she felt an urgency in the force that held her there. An urgency that almost took her breath away.

And she felt a *presence*. A presence that was telling her without words, without even the hissing sounds of silence she'd heard before, that *something was coming. Something terrible.*

Be aware. Be ready.

And then she heard the whimpering of a dog beneath her window.

19

Afterward, when it was over, Kathy looked at the clock.

Only a few minutes had elapsed. It had seemed an eternity.

Kathy lay in the dark, alert and unafraid now.

Fear, she realized, either pushes you to the point where you lose your reason, or to a point even beyond that, where there is no fear, and you become coldly rational.

The latter had happened to her.

The dog had stopped whimpering when the cold left the room and the pressure on her body lifted. Kathy wasn't surprised. She knew now where that dog came from.

No wonder her parents had never heard it, those other times, just as they had never felt the cold on the landing.

And no wonder she hadn't seen it when she'd gone to her window and looked down. She wasn't able to see the seated bodies of the murdered Mrs. Winston and her two sons on the landing, either.

The dog, she realized now, was a part of the hauntings. It was the one Mr. Winston had killed ten years ago out there on the deck.

And she was sure now that it was what she'd heard whimpering on the landing the night she'd screamed and frightened her parents. First she'd heard it on the deck and then on the landing—the two places associated with its death.

The dog had been on the landing the night of the murders, Matt had said. It must have followed Mr. Winston when he carried the stiffening bodies of his victims up the stairs and propped them against the wall.

Kathy loved dogs. She knew how they behaved. Maybe the little dog had been trying to rouse Mrs. Winston and the children. Mitzi used to do that. She'd crawl up on Kathy's bed when Kathy was sleeping and nudge her with her nose in an attempt to awaken her.

Had the dog—a small black and white Border collie, Matt said—been trying, with growing desperation, to bring life back into the bodies of Mrs. Winston and her sons?

It had probably been whimpering around the bodies, nudging and prodding them, when Mr. Winston decided to kill it, too.

And then it had fled, bleeding, through the house, only to be caught and butchered on the deck.

But why all this paranormal activity tonight with the dog and the Winstons?

Yes, the Winstons. She realized this was the first time she'd allowed herself to put a name to the listeners. It had to be the Winstons, the mother and her sons. Who else would be inhabiting the landing, silent and listening, chilling it with their terrible memories?

What were they listening for? And why, tonight, did they invade her room, surrounding her with those feelings of impending danger?

Had the anxiety about Philip's disappearance triggered it, the way a dying echo is reinforced by someone calling the word again?

She had to talk to someone about this. She couldn't carry the burden alone much longer.

No use going to her parents. They were upset about Philip. They would be impatient with her and tell her she was only imagining things again.

No, it would have to be Matt. They'd become so close. They had so much in common. Their minds seemed to run on the same track. Surely he would understand. She'd make him understand. And together they would decide what needed to be done to rid the house of these hauntings.

There were people—parapsychologists—who dealt with this sort of thing. She'd seen a program about them on TV. Maybe she and Matt could find one and talk to him.

Yes, she would tell Matt everything, starting with the first time she'd set foot on the landing. She would tell him about the cold, and her feeling that someone was there, listening. And the dog. And about this latest happening, the unspoken warning of danger she'd just received.

Matt would help her. She could always count on him.

"It's probably my fault you're having these feelings, Kathy," Matt said slowly. "I shouldn't have described every last detail of those murders. And now, thanks to me, you've been imagining those bodies on the landing, and the dead dog and—"

"But I'm not imagining them, Matt. That's what I've been trying to tell you. They're real."

She took a breath and tried again.

"I'm not saying I'm psychic or have supernatural gifts or anything. And I've never had ESP. That's what I don't understand. And yet, I swear to you, Matt, I'm not imagining this. I wanted it to go away. I thought maybe it would. But it hasn't. And it's getting worse."

They were sitting at a picnic table in the park that overlooked Brentwood Lake. The park was deserted. Few people came here once summer ended.

A cold, gusting wind ruffled the dark surface of the lake and blew dead leaves against the legs of the table. Overhead, the bare branches of the trees rattled in the wind, like skeleton fingers.

Kathy shivered.

"Would you like to go back to the car?" Matt asked.

"No, not until we've talked this out, Matt."

Matt looked beyond her, to the lake. "Okay,

let's analyze the problem, then. You said you were pretty unhappy about the move, right?"

Kathy nodded. "Yes, but—"

"And the first time you came into the house, you were tired. You'd been traveling all day, you said."

"I wasn't *that* tired," Kathy said defensively.

"And you went up on the landing and you felt the cold."

Matt turned to her. "Kathy, it was cold when you came to Brentwood. Your house had sat empty for months. Or if the front door was open when you went up the stairs, there could have been a draft on the landing. Maybe that was the cold you felt."

"You don't understand," Kathy said desperately. "This wasn't a normal cold. It's hard to explain it if you've never experienced it."

"And right after you moved in," Matt continued, "you discovered you were living in a house where a family had been murdered. How did you feel about that?"

"I was horrified, of course. I wanted to move, but my folks talked to me and explained things and then I calmed down."

"Calmed down? Then you *were* pretty upset. So maybe—"

"Stop!" Kathy jumped up from the picnic bench, her fists clenched.

"I didn't come here to be analyzed, Matt. I told you, I've tried and tried to explain things to myself, finding reasons for everything, but it hasn't worked. Don't you understand what I'm saying? Can't you see? There are things happening to me in that house that can't be explained rationally."

Matt stood up slowly, his expression guarded. "So what you're saying, Kathy, is that your house is haunted."

"Yes, I guess that's what I'm saying. That murdered family wants something from me, and I don't know what it is."

Kathy hated the way Matt was looking at her. She hated the pity and the disbelief in his eyes.

"You don't believe me, do you?" she asked coldly. "Or maybe you think I'm crazy. Is that it, Matt? Are you afraid you've hooked yourself up with a loony?"

"No, of course not. It's just that—"

Kathy snatched up her carryall and threw it over her shoulder.

"I'd like to go home now, Matt."

"Wait, Kathy. We haven't finished talking."

"I think we've both said just about as much as we're ever going to say to each other."

"What do you mean?" Matt's face was pale.

"I mean that it was really nice while it lasted, Matt, but you're not the person I thought you were."

Now it was Matt's turn to lose his temper. "You're saying it's over between us because I don't go along with your story about ghosts?"

"No, it's over because you refused to listen to what I was trying to tell you."

"I listened, but it didn't make any sense.

You're being imaginative and hysterical, that's what's happening."

"Hysterical? How dare you say I'm hysterical!"

"Well, look at you right now, Kathy. There's no reasoning with you."

Kathy marched over to the car and flung open the door on her side.

She turned and fired her last shot at Matt.

"I'm sorry we don't have our class rings. I'm sorry I'm not wearing yours around my neck."

"Why?"

"So I could rip it off and throw it at you. Now, will you please take me home?"

No one noticed Kathy's black depression at supper. They were too busy talking about Philip's disappearance.

The police hadn't found Philip in the woods. And Sergeant Martin had come by the house in the afternoon with bad news.

"We checked every school in Brentwood today, public and private, and drew a complete blank, Mrs. Colby. There's no one who looks like Philip or answers to his description in any of them."

"But that's impossible," Mrs. Colby had said. "Surely he has to go to school somewhere."

"We checked the surrounding neighborhoods, too, and no one seems to have heard of the boy."

"Then where did he come from?"

"I don't know," Sergeant Martin replied. "And that photo isn't much help. It's rather faded and blurry, as you well know. As far as we can determine, your son is the only person who knows anything about Philip."

"Oh . . ." said Mrs. Colby in a faint, stricken voice.

"Is there something you feel you should tell me?" Sergeant Martin asked. "Something you haven't mentioned before?"

"No, not really," Mrs. Colby said hesitantly. "It's only that . . . well, in the past, my son has had a series of imaginary friends and . . . "

"Are you saying there's a possibility that Philip might not be a real child?" Sergeant Martin's voice was sharp.

Mrs. Colby threw out her hands. "No. Of course not. Philip's real. We have his photo, don't we? And Timothy insists Philip is *not* an imaginary friend. I know we can believe him. In the past, he has always admitted when they weren't real."

"I see," Sergeant Martin said, rubbing his chin thoughtfully.

"I hope this doesn't mean you intend to give up your search, Officer."

"No, not for a while at least. We'll keep a bulletin out on him, but I can't promise you anything. We have no proof of the boy's existence beyond what your son has told you, backed up only by an old photo that could have come from anywhere."

As he left, Sergeant Martin paused to caution, "I hope you realize that, under the circumstances, we must proceed with extreme caution in this investigation. We don't want to cause an outbreak of mass hysteria here in Brentwood, if there is any possibility this child exists only in your son's mind."

Mrs. Colby nodded. "I know you are all doing your best, Officer Martin. But I do feel strongly that Philip truly exists. Maybe he'll show up here. If and when he does, I'll call you immediately."

"Thank you," said Sergeant Martin. "I'd appreciate it. But try not to get your hopes up, Mrs. Colby."

"But Philip *is* real," Timmy insisted when his mother had related her conversation with Sergeant Martin. "He's *not* 'maginary!"

"You're sure, darling? You're absolutely, positively sure?"

Timmy drew a large *X* on his chest. "Cross my heart and hope to die," he said solemnly.

For some strange reason, his childish vow made Kathy shiver. *Maybe Matt is right. Maybe I am becoming irrational about this house.*

There was more bad news.

"I tried to change the dates on that out-of-town trip I'm booked for," her father said, "but it's no use. The meetings have all been set up. Too much is involved, Marian. I've got to leave tomorrow morning. Early."

"Oh no," Mrs. Colby moaned. "Any time but now."

"I'm sorry, but there's nothing I can do. I'll only be gone three days."

"Of course," Mrs. Colby said, giving herself a

brisk shake. "I understand. And there's really nothing you can do here, anyway. I'll call you at your hotel if we hear anything more about Philip."

Kathy could hardly wait to be alone that night, and in bed, so she could cry without being overheard.

Her life here in Brentwood was hopeless. Impossible. First, this horrible house. Then Philip's disappearance. And now her fight with Matt.

It had only been a few hours since they'd parted and she missed him already. He hadn't said anything to her in the car, either. She'd hoped he'd tell her he was sorry, that he really did believe her after all, that he understood, but he hadn't.

And he hadn't looked at her or said anything when he'd dropped her off at the house. She'd been hoping, right up to the last, that he would.

And now it was over between them.

She pulled her covers over her head, preparing herself for a good, long cry.

If anything hissed or moved or whimpered on the landing that night, she didn't intend to hear it.

20

It was even worse the next morning.

Matt called while she was eating breakfast.

"Look, Kathy—maybe, under the circumstances, you'd prefer I didn't pick you up this morning."

His voice was polite but unreadable.

Kathy thought quickly. What did he mean? Was he trying to get out of seeing her, or was he merely putting the ball in her court?

And if she said *yes, please pick me up, Matt,* would he think she'd backed down on how she felt? That she was willing to say she was just a foolish, hysterical, stupid woman?

Or did he want to pick her up so he could tell her he was sorry, and that he understood, now, what she'd been trying to tell him?

Not likely, she decided. If he felt that way, he would have said so. And not in that cold, super-polite voice, either.

Aloud she said, "Maybe you're right, Matt. Maybe you shouldn't pick me up today."

She sat next to him in homeroom, but they didn't speak much. They only said what was absolutely necessary to preserve civility. She did, however, get a savage satisfaction from the fact that he looked pretty awful. As if he hadn't slept much.

Of course, she didn't look all that great herself. Cold compresses on her eyes this morning hadn't removed all the puffiness caused by her crying jag last night.

She skipped lunch. How could she face the staff of the *Brentwood Bugle*? They'd know something was wrong right away, and how would she react? Besides, Matt wasn't outside the biology lab, waiting to walk her to the cafeteria.

That was the very worst moment she had all day. She hadn't realized how important it was to find him waiting for her, his grey eyes lighting up when she came through the door and smiled at him.

Once, when they passed in the hall, Matt had stopped dead and started to say something to her, but she turned her head and kept going.

Dumb! Dumb! she told herself, even as she went past him. Yet what else could she do? Something important was at stake here. His belief in her. Her belief in her own integrity.

The other shoe dropped at dinner when the phone rang.

It was Aunt Janet, Mrs. Colby's sister, calling from the hospital in Minnesota, where she lived. She needed emergency surgery. Could Marian come and ride herd on her young children—all four of them—until arrangements could be made for a live-in sitter?

"I'm desperate, Marian," Aunt Janet said, "really desperate or I wouldn't ask you to do this. It will be only for a couple of days, max. Ted's been phoning agencies to get someone here pronto, but in the meantime . . . "

"Are you sure you'll be able to manage without me, Kathy?" Mrs. Colby asked as she threw clothes into her overnighter.

"You know I will Mom. I can cook. I'm a good cook. And I've been baby-sitting Timmy since he was born."

"But . . . you'll be alone here. What if something, God forbid, should happen?"

"What can happen? In an emergency I can always dial 911."

"I mean about Philip," her mother said.

"I've got Sergeant Martin's number, Mom. He said he'd let us know if they found out anything."

"You have your father's hotel number, in case you can't reach me?"

"Yes, yes! So go. Don't worry!"

"I should be back Monday afternoon at the latest," Mrs. Colby said. "But don't forget to—"

"I'll get Timmy off to school. Don't worry Mom. Everything's going to be fine. Just fine."

*   *   *

Kathy had been cheerful only for her mother's benefit. Actually, she was worried.

This was the worst possible time for her parents to go off and leave her and Timothy, she thought.

First, there was that business about Philip. Yes, Mom had left Sergeant Martin's phone number, but . . .

But—and this was what worried her more than anything else—what about that feeling of impending danger she'd received the other night from The Listeners? That was what she called them now. It was too painful, too frightening, to think of them as Mrs. Winston and her sons. What kind of danger did they mean? And when would it happen?

If only I can hang tight until Dad returns. Only a day and a half, now, until he comes home.

I wish Matt was still around.

Oh, Matt. I really miss you!

21

Saturday afternoon and Timmy was moping.

Kathy had done her best all day to entertain him—cartoons, games, his favorite lunch—but it hadn't worked. Timmy was worried about Philip.

"What do you think his daddy will do to him?" he asked.

"Nothing," she said, lying. "His daddy won't hurt him. I know he won't."

"So where is he, then?" Timothy persisted.

"Somewhere safe, I'm sure. Maybe at an aunt's house. Or an uncle's." Kathy's voice sounded false, overly cheerful, even to herself. "Don't worry, Timmy. Philip's okay."

But is he? she wondered. *Where is he, and what's happening to him? And will the police be able to find him before his father does?*

Kathy gathered up the Lego blocks left over from the skyscraper they'd been building and threw them into a box. "Listen, Timmy," she said with a hasty glance at her watch. "I need to do some work at the library before it closes. I have a term paper to write for world history and I haven't even started it yet. Will you be okay for a couple of hours without me?"

"Will I be here all alone?" Timmy asked fearfully.

Philip said it was a bad house. Was it starting to affect Timmy, too?

"No, of course not, darling. I've got Mrs. Metzger coming in a few minutes. You know her. She's sat with you before."

"Oh, her. Yeah, she was real nice," Timmy answered. "Do you think she'll let me play in my tree house?"

"I don't know why not," Kathy said, "but isn't it a little too cold today to play out there?"

Timmy looked out the window. It was a grey, sunless day. And now it had begun to drizzle. He squared his small shoulders and said resolutely, "Yes, but I thought if I stayed up in the tree house, Philip might see me and come back."

Kathy passed Dennis as she drove down the street. He was trimming some bushes for Mrs. Jergens, the elderly widow who lived at the end of the block.

He stopped his work and watched Kathy as she went by. She glanced in the rear view mirror as she turned the corner. He was still watching her.

What a weirdo, Kathy thought. *Down deep, though, he's probably just a nice old guy, trying to make an honest living.*

"But he still gives me the creeps!" she added aloud.

*   *   *

The man watched her until she was out of sight. Then he gathered up his clippers and rake and stowed them in the back of his van. He didn't bother to collect his day's wages from Mrs. Jergens. None of this mattered any more. His work here was at an end.

This was the sign he'd been waiting for.

Last night, the white light had come to him and The Voices said that if he saw the girl with Estelle's silver-gilt hair today, it meant the time had come.

The sacred time that would fulfill Their prophecy.

The time when Philip must die.

"You'll find everything we have on the Wars of the Roses in this section," said the librarian.

"Thank you," Kathy said with a heavy sigh. "I almost wish you didn't have quite so much!"

The librarian laughed. "It's not as complicated as it seems, once you get the families sorted out."

Kathy gathered up a large armload of books, sat down at a quiet table behind the book stacks and began reading. Why had she picked this topic? The wars were so long ago. So pointless. Cousins killing cousins to gain control of the throne of England. What a waste!

Almost against her will she found herself wondering about the Winston murders.

The library must have all the back issues of

the local newspaper right here, on microfilm. Should she . . . ?

No, she'd promised her mother.

But Mom didn't know anything about those signals she was getting from the landing. Wasn't it just plain stupid to keep going without knowing the full facts about the murders?

Maybe she could find something in the newspaper accounts that would help her understand what was happening.

The librarian loaded the first roll into one of the microfilm readers.

"This doesn't have anything to do with the Wars of the Roses," she said.

"I know," Kathy said, not meeting her eyes. "I . . . I might change the subject of my term paper."

"This is a bit sensational for a term paper, isn't it?" asked the librarian. "Well, never mind. Now, here's how you go forward, and this is how you reverse. Got that? This roll should cover the first few days following the discovery of the bodies. As I recall, those murders caused quite a stir here in Brentwood. I don't believe they ever caught the murderer."

"No," Kathy said, her eyes on the screen. "But most people think he's dead."

"If you need any further help, just let me know," said the librarian as she left. "I still think you ought to stick with the Wars of the Roses, though."

"You're probably right," Kathy said, smiling weakly.

As soon as she was alone, Kathy forwarded the film, scanning it closely until she came to the report of the murders.

FOREIGN SERVICE OFFICER KILLS WIFE AND SONS, the banner headline read. Beneath that, a smaller headline added, MURDERER STILL AT LARGE.

The front page showed a picture of Mr. Winston. It was obviously an official ID photo. He was dressed in a dark three-piece suit and was smiling pleasantly into the camera. His hair was close-cropped, almost a military haircut, and his skin shone with health.

He doesn't look like a murderer, Kathy thought. Not like someone who could kill his own family.

And here was a picture of the victims.

She leaned closer to the machine. The wife, Estelle, and her young sons were standing on the deck—*the deck of her house!*—laughing and squinting into the sun. The littlest boy peeped shyly, half hidden, from behind his mother's skirt. A small black and white dog sat at their feet.

The little dog. The one who . . .

They looked so happy. Even the dog. It sat up so pert, so erect, its mouth open in a doggie smile. One of the boys had his hand on the dog's back in a caressing gesture.

Kathy shuddered. Thank God they hadn't known what was coming.

Mr. Winston must have taken those pictures. What had he been thinking as he lined them up in the camera? Was he planning, even then, to kill them?

Estelle was lovely, Kathy noted. Slim and small-boned, with long blonde hair. In this photo, she was wearing it in a thick braid that hung over one shoulder.

It was hard to see their faces distinctly in the newspaper photo, but, even so, Kathy could see that the boys resembled their mother. Pale blonde. Fair complexioned. Slender.

Why, Timmy and I could almost be related to them! Kathy thought in sudden amazement. *Same color hair. Same body build.*

How strange. Maybe this odd resemblance was one reason she was being contacted by The Listeners. Maybe they felt a kinship to her or something.

At the bottom of the newspaper was another photo, this time a close-up.

BODY OF YOUNGEST CHILD FOUND IN BACKYARD said the caption beneath it.

A grey haze passed before Kathy's eyes as she stared at the photo, and she felt as if a massive hand had just taken hold of her heart, squeezing it, squeezing it so tightly that it stopped beating. Her ears rang and for a moment she was afraid she might fall over in a faint.

And then the haze cleared and her heart began beating again. Kathy found she was shaking so violently, so uncontrollably, that she had to clamp a hand to her jaw to stop its spastic jerking.

The picture of the youngest child, the one who was not found with the bodies on the landing . . . the one who was found in the backyard . . .

The newspaper said his name was Philip.

Philip. Seven years old, according to the newspaper. He'd celebrated his birthday shortly before the tragedy.

She recognized him. How could she not recognize him?

The hair. The pale little face. His resemblance to Timothy.

Philip. The youngest Winston child.

Philip, Timmy's friend.

Oh my God—My God! It was Philip!

22

She barely remembered driving home.

She roared into the garage, punched the button that closed the garage doors and ran into the house through the side entrance.

Mrs. Metzger stood up as Kathy came into the living room.

"I'm so glad you're home early, dear," she said, reaching for her coat which was draped over the sofa. "I do need to leave. I just got a call from my son, and he wants me to—"

"Sure, Mrs. Metzger, you can leave now," Kathy said breathlessly. "But where's Timmy?"

"Up in his tree house," said Mrs. Metzger, shrugging herself into her coat.

"He went there soon after you left. I've been going down to the fishpond and calling up to him from time to time to make sure he's all right, and he seems to be just fine."

She paused in the act of tying a filmy chiffon scarf around her neck. "Is anything wrong, dear? You look terribly pale."

"No . . . no, I'm fine." Kathy pawed through her carryall in search of her wallet. "Let's see now, how much do I owe you?"

Mrs. Metzger put her purse over her arm and headed for the front door. "Don't bother. I'll get it from your mother when she returns from her trip. Oh, and by the way, Kathy, I'm so glad to see that Timothy is making friends now."

"Friends? What friends?" Kathy asked.

"Well, one friend, anyway," Mrs. Metzger said as she opened the door. "Up there in the tree house with him. I could hear them talking."

"Did you see him, Mrs. Metzger? Timmy's friend?"

"No, but Timmy was talking to someone a few minutes ago, when I last checked on him. Really, Kathy, you do look like you're coming down with something. You're as pale as a ghost."

When the door closed on Mrs. Metzger, Kathy ran through the house and out the back door. Then down the sloping length of the back lawn to the fishpond and the tree house.

"Timmy!" she cried as she ran. "Timmy!"

She was breathless when she arrived at the big oak tree.

The rope ladder was hanging down from the tree house. Good. Timmy hadn't pulled it up as he sometimes did.

As she scrambled up the ladder, Kathy heard voices. Or was it just one voice—Timmy's? He seemed to be having a conversation with someone.

Who?

She finally reached the top rung. But even as her head cleared the platform, she knew there would be no one with Timothy in the tree house.

She was right. Timothy was alone. He was sitting on his rolled up sleeping bag, and he looked angry.

"Timmy," she gasped. "Who were you talking to?"

"Philip. He was here. Now he's gone. You scared him away."

He glared at her. "He wasn't here very long, either. I kept asking and asking him where he'd been, but he said he couldn't tell me. It was a secret place, he said. His mother and big brothers were there. He says they're all scared about what his daddy is going to do. He was just starting to tell me about it when he heard you coming. It was something really important, too."

Kathy had begun to tremble again, the way she had in the library. She was trembling so violently she could hardly cling to the ladder. Gripping the rope with both hands she said, "I heard you talking to him when I was climbing up here. How could he have left the tree house without my seeing him? Where did he go?"

Timothy looked puzzled. "I don't know, Kathy. He just comes and goes. I'll look up and he's just . . . there."

"Come on, Timmy," Kathy said, backing down the ladder, her legs shaking on the rungs. "Let's go to the house. We have to talk."

"But I want to stay up here. Maybe Philip will come back."

"No. You come down right this minute," his sister snapped. "And that's an order!"

Timmy was shivering with the cold when Kathy got him to the house, so she sat him in the kitchen and fixed a pot of hot cocoa.

The overcast, drizzly day was turning to twilight. The sky was already a flat, greyish purple, and the bare, wintry limbs of the trees were black and stark, like pen drawings, against the cold sky.

"We've got to talk about Philip," Kathy said, sitting opposite Timothy and wrapping her hands around the steaming mug of cocoa. She had to hold the mug in both hands as she drank. They were still unsteady, and the rim of the mug rattled against her teeth.

"But I've told you everything," Timmy complained. "What more do you want to know?"

"This is important, Timmy. Really important," she told him. "You must tell me the truth. Do you understand?"

He nodded, his eyes wide.

A possible explanation of the Philip riddle had come to her as she fixed the cocoa. This was it. It had to be it. The alternative was too horrible. Too unbelievable. Her brother, playing with a ghost? The ghost of a murdered little boy? No. It simply could not be.

"Okay," she said, setting down her cocoa mug. "Here's the question. When you found the picture of Philip in the tree house, do you think maybe you thought about him so much that he started to seem like a real person to you? And maybe that's why you only play with him in the tree house—because that's where the picture was. And you knew his name because it was written on the back of the picture."

"I told you and I told you," Timmy said angrily, slamming down his mug and spilling his cocoa. "Philip is real. I don't have 'maginary friends any more."

"Maybe you don't *think* he's imaginary, but—"

"No!" Timothy shook his head violently. "Philip isn't like any of my 'maginary friends. That's cause he's real! And besides, all that stuff on the back of the picture was written in cursive. I don't know how to read cursive. So how did I know his name if he didn't tell me?"

"Do . . . do you know anything else about him?" Kathy asked cautiously.

"Yeah. He has two brothers. They're with his mommy. He likes his brothers, but they used to tease him a lot. And he has a little black dog named Roxie. She's with his mommy, too."

He paused, trying to remember more. "Oh yeah, his mommy has this real pretty name. I can't remember what it is, but it sounds like Esther or something."

Kathy's mouth was so dry she had to lick her lips before she could speak. "Was her name . . . Estelle?"

"Yes, that's it, Kathy. How'd you know? Philip only told *me* that this afternoon, and I'm his best friend."

Kathy went through the house, snapping on all the lights, pushing back the dark.

She intended to leave the lights on all night. And she and Timothy would sleep in her parents' king-sized bed, with the TV going all night, too. She'd tell him it was a party, and that she'd make popcorn. He'd like that.

And then, first thing tomorrow morning, she would call Mrs. Metzger and ask her if she would come and live in the house with her and Timmy until their parents got home.

She'd say she was sick. The flu. Hadn't Mrs. Metzger told her how pale she looked?

And then, when her folks got home, she'd tell them everything. They'd have to believe her now. She'd take them to the library and show them Philip's photo in the newspaper.

They had to do something about this house. Surely they would see that now. They could call in a parapsychologist. Or an exorcist, if it came to that. And if that didn't work, they would have to move, just like all the others who had lived here before them.

Mom wouldn't need much coaxing to do that, once she found out that her son's best friend was a ghost!

Timmy had stopped talking about Philip at supper. He was too excited about spending the night in his parents' bed, watching TV and staying up as late as he wanted to.

Kathy had fixed Timothy his favorite meal—creamed mushrooms on toast. And then she'd filled the tub for him and made him take a long, hot soak. He was up in their parents' big bed now, with a bowl of popcorn and a cola. She'd carried Mitzi upstairs and dumped her on the bed with Timmy. The two of them seemed to be enjoying themselves. Timmy was happily clicking the remote control while Mitzi had trampled out a cozy nest for herself among the quilts.

"I'll be up in a little bit," Kathy said as she left the room.

"Hurry," Timmy said. "There's a cowboy movie on next."

Kathy went back to the kitchen and put the dishes in the sink. She'd worry about them tomorrow.

Then she sat down at the kitchen table, her hands pressed to her temples.

Should she call her parents?

No. There was no way she could explain all this over the phone. Besides, her mother would want to come home right away, and Aunt Janet needed her. And Dad's new job depended on this big meeting.

There was only one person she could talk to now. Matt.

But would he want to talk to her if she called?

*   *   *

The man was hiding in the bushes by the kitchen door.

He checked his belt to make sure he hadn't forgotten his hunting knife. He'd sharpened it carefully, lovingly, on a stone, honing it to a razor-fine edge. He couldn't use poison this time, so he'd have to do it the way the prophets of old sacrificed their sheep, and he needed a sharp knife for that.

He wouldn't fail Them this time.

He'd arrived at his vantage point in the woods just in time to see Philip come down the tree house ladder. The girl with the pale hair had been waiting for him at the bottom and had practically dragged him up the length of the lawn to the house.

As soon as it got dark, the man had edged closer to the house. He had to make sure Philip was still there.

Yes, he was there all right, just as The Voices had promised. From behind a tree, he watched as lights came on all over the house. Good. That made it easier to see what they were up to. First he'd seen Philip in the kitchen, and then in some of the rooms upstairs. And now he was in the master bedroom—his and Estelle's old room.

He shook his head to clear his brain. Mustn't think of Estelle now. He had to concentrate on what he needed to do to Philip.

Funny about Philip. He was sure Philip had died that last time. He'd even read about it in the papers.

Maybe it had been a trick to make sure he

wouldn't come back and kill Philip. That was probably it. And it had worked, hadn't it?

Yes, but he knew better now.

And in a few short minutes he would right the wrong and do what should have been done ten years ago.

23

Kathy reached for the wall phone and dialed Matt's number.

What if he refused to speak to her? That was a terrible thing she'd done to him yesterday at school—snubbing him like that when he tried to talk to her.

Or maybe he was out on a date. After all, it *was* Saturday night and there were lots of girls at Brentwood High dying to snag Matt Hamilton.

The phone rang once. Twice. And then Matt answered.

"Matt," Kathy said. "Please don't hang up. It's me, Kathy."

"Kathy!" The joy in his voice was unmistakable. "Kathy! I tried to get you this afternoon, but the baby-sitter said you were out and—"

"Oh Matt, I'm so glad to hear your voice. I've missed you so." She laughed, giddy with relief. "I know it's only been a day and a half since we broke up, but I've missed you."

"Me too," Matt said. "And then yesterday when you . . . Well, I thought maybe you were through with me forever."

Kathy clutched the receiver tightly and closed her eyes so she could concentrate on what she was saying. "Listen, Matt. I've got to talk to you. Something's happened—something important. Both my folks are out of town. I really need you. Can you come over?"

"Sure I can. Are you okay? Has something happened to Timothy?"

Kathy shook her head, even though Matt couldn't see her. "No. It has something to do with what I was trying to tell you before."

A brief pause. She wondered what he was thinking. Then his voice came, strong and reassuring. "Look, Kathy, I'm afraid I didn't give you much of a chance the last time. But I've been doing a lot of thinking since then, and I did some reading on the subject of paranormal experiences at the library yesterday. I'll be a better listener this time around."

"Oh Matt, I can't tell you how much better you make me feel. When can you get here?"

"I'll be there right away. Just take it easy."

"Okay, and—wait a minute. Don't hang up."

"Why? What's wrong, Kathy?"

"Sssh! I heard a funny noise on the back porch. *Matt—I think someone's out there!*"

Still clutching the phone, she ducked behind the open door of the pantry. From here she could watch the back door without being seen herself.

The sound came again. A stealthy shuffling sound.

She looked up at the window over the door and gasped.

"Kathy? What is it? What's going on?"

"Matt," she whispered. "There's a man . . . it's Dennis . . . that awful old handyman I told you about. He's looking in the window!"

"Can he see you?"

"No. Not now, but maybe he did before. Oh God, Matt, now he's rattling the door. He's trying to get in!"

"Where's Timothy?"

"Upstairs."

"Then listen to me, Kathy. Hang up the phone. I'll dial 911. You get yourself and Timmy into an upstairs bedroom and lock the door. Do you hear me? Hang up the phone—you might need to dial out from upstairs—and then lock yourself in a bedroom."

Kathy laid the phone down quietly on the floor, breaking the connection.

Dennis must know she was in the pantry. The phone cord stretched from the wall by the sink to where she was standing. How could she get out of the kitchen without him seeing her?

From behind the cover of the open pantry door, she moved stealthily, her back to the wall, toward the door leading to the dining room. When she was only a few steps away, she made a break for it.

The rattling at the back door was getting more violent. Would the door hold until she got upstairs?

Kathy took the steps two at a time.

The cold on the landing was so intense she was almost paralyzed.

And the sounds! Distant, muffled sobbing. A woman's. And then the hopeless, despairing wails of young children coming toward her as if funneled down a long, echoing corridor. And the dog . . . it was up here, too, whimpering with fear.

The freezing cold pressed against her.

She tried to move.

And then she heard the sound of breaking glass.

Dennis was getting in! He'd broken the window over the kitchen door. What would he do to her and Timmy? He must have seen Mom and Dad carrying suitcases when they left. He knew they were alone in the house.

Almost alone. Suddenly she felt cold hands pushing her, urging her forward. Were they trying to protect her? If only they could.

But at least they got her moving again. She ran down the hall, into the master bedroom, slamming and locking the door behind her.

The door was solid, but the little push button lock wouldn't keep *him* out for very long.

She dragged a small chest over in front of the door. It was the best she could do.

Timmy was staring at her, open mouthed. "Kathy! What are you doing?"

She crossed the floor in long strides and threw back the bedcovers. Timmy's bathrobe was on the floor beside the bed. She snatched it up and pulled it around him, grabbing his arms roughly and thrusting them into the sleeves.

"Ouch, Kathy—you're hurting me."

Kathy lowered her face to his level. "Listen to me, Timmy. You're going to have to be a really big boy. We're in trouble. A bad man is in the house, and I think he wants to hurt us. The police are coming, but until they get here, we can't let him come near us. Understand?"

Timmy nodded, all eyes.

"Sssh, listen!" Kathy commanded, her finger on her lips.

He was coming up the stairs. She could hear his feet. He was walking slowly but heavily, as if he were sure he had all the time in the world.

An old ghost story, one she'd heard many times around Girl Scout campfires, flashed into Kathy's mind. In it, the ghost, tromping up the stairs, lusting for vengeance, calls out, "I'm on the first step . . . I'm on the second step . . . "

Only that's not what *he* was calling.

"Philip!" he called. "Philip? Are you there? Answer Daddy."

Timmy shuddered. "It's Philip's father," he whispered. "Philip said he would come back to hurt him."

But Philip was dead. Philip wasn't here!

And then the jolting adrenaline of fear caused Kathy's mind to function in triple time.

Philip's father . . . the missing Charles Winston. They never caught him. They thought he was dead.

But what if he wasn't?

He had to be crazy to do the things he'd done. Killer crazy. And now he was after Philip.

Why? Didn't he know he killed Philip ten years ago?

Wait . . . maybe he didn't know Philip was dead. Timmy looked just like Philip. Maybe he thought Timmy was Philip.

That was it. He wanted to kill Philip again.

Only this time he'd be killing Timmy!

"Phi-lip! Daddy's coming!"

He'd have to cross the landing. The Listeners . . . could they stop him?

No. He was too powerful for them, consumed as he was by his murderous insanity. He probably wouldn't even sense their presence.

I'm on my own, Kathy thought desperately.

She grabbed Timmy and ran toward the adjoining master bath.

"Wait!" Timmy said, wrenching himself free. "Mitzi!"

Kathy remembered the little black and white Border collie. No, she couldn't let Dennis . . . Charles Winston . . . kill Mitzi the way he'd killed that other poor dog.

She ran back to the bed and pulled Mitzi from the covers. Mitzi woke up and uttered a startled yelp as she was dragged from her warm nest.

"Come on, Timmy," Kathy urged, tucking Mitzi under her arm like a football. "Into the bathroom."

She locked the bathroom door behind them. Another stupid little push button lock.

Please, God, let the police get here soon!

She put her ear to the door. She could hear

him. He was outside in the hall, throwing himself at the bedroom door. It wouldn't be long, now, before that feeble little lock gave. And then a few more minutes and he'd have the bathroom door open, too. And they'd be trapped in here, like mice.

Oh no, we won't.

She looked around quickly. The bathroom window. They could squeeze through the window and climb out onto the roof.

But what about Mitzi? If they left her here, she'd be butchered. No. Never!

A pair of Mrs. Colby's black cotton tights was hanging over the shower stall. Kathy pulled them down in one quick motion and stuffed the bewildered Mitzi into the seat part of them.

Then she took the legs and bound them around her waist. By pulling them tight, she could get them around her several times, securing Mitzi close against her, like a baby kangaroo in a pouch.

Mitzi was wheezing a protest when Kathy lifted Timmy and boosted him through the small, narrow bathroom window.

Timmy was pale, even paler than usual, but he wasn't crying. His little jaw was set and he scrambled through the window without a murmur.

He's trying to be a big boy, Kathy thought. *I'll love him forever for this. If we make it.*

She had to stand on the toilet tank to get out the window, but she made it, even with Mitzi strapped to her.

The roof was steeply pitched—funny she'd

never noticed just how steep it really was—and she had a brief but terrifying moment of vertigo as she stepped out on it. Timmy was clinging to the incline like a little monkey. He didn't look frightened now. This was his element. His one talent. Climbing.

"We have to get down to the ground, Timmy," she told him. "If we stay here, he'll crawl out and get us. And then once on the ground, we're going to have to run for help, okay?"

"Okay," Timmy said.

"Listen to me, Timmy, and try to remember what I'm saying. You're not to worry about me. No matter what happens, I want you to run just as fast as you can, okay?"

Timmy eyes shone with tears in the moonlight. "I . . . I couldn't do that, Kathy. I couldn't just run away and leave you. You're my sister. I love you."

Kathy blinked back her own tears and said, "Then prove it by saving yourself, darling. I love you, too."

Surprisingly, it was Timothy who talked Kathy down the steep incline of the roof onto the lower, flatter pitch of the garage.

They heard Dennis burst into the bedroom as they lowered themselves cautiously to the top of the fence and then onto the garbage cans.

He was throwing himself at the bathroom door now. They could hear him clearly through the open window.

And then, as Kathy turned to jump down

from the garbage can, she slipped. The can rolled over with a clatter and she fell to the ground. For a moment, she was not sure if she could rise.

Mitzi had survived the fall, that was certain. She was yelping and struggling against the pantyhose that bound her, and Kathy felt a warm wetness against her abdomen. In all the excitement, Mitzi had piddled.

Timothy tugged at Kathy's arm. "Hurry, Kathy. He's looking at us!"

Dennis—Charles Winston—was at the bathroom window, staring down at them. "Come back, Philip! Wait for Daddy!"

Kathy dragged herself to her feet. The windows of the closest house were dark. No one home.

She knew the neighbors on the other side were out of town. Her mother had mentioned it a couple of days ago. Farther—much farther down the street, a light shone dimly in the window of Mrs. Jergens, the elderly widow.

Kathy thought quickly. They could probably outrun *him*, but would he catch them when they were on the porch, waiting for Mrs. Jergens to open up? Mrs. Jergens used a walker and it took forever for her to come to the door.

And even if they did get inside before he caught up with them, her door was one of those old-fashioned ones, with the large oval of plated glass. He—Dennis—could break that with no trouble and then Mrs. Jergens would be endangered, too.

The family car was in the garage, but Kathy

didn't have her keys. Besides, she couldn't get the garage doors open from outside without the electronic device.

Dennis's head disappeared from the bathroom window. Where was he now? What should they do?

For the rest of her life, Kathy would never forget what happened next.

"Look, Kathy," Timothy cried, pointing. "It's Philip!"

The moon cast pale, wavering fingers of light through the trees. Was that fading gleam Timmy pointed to a trick of the moonlight, or the trembling ghost of a boy with silver-blonde hair?

"He says, 'come on'," Timmy urged. "He wants us to come to the tree house."

The tree house! Of course! It was their only chance. They could beat Dennis—*Mr. Winston*— there in the dark. Timmy knew every rock and stone in the path. And once they reached the safety of the platform, they could pull up the rope ladder and await the arrival of the police, who should be here soon.

Kathy grabbed Timmy's hand and they ran around the house and down the lawn toward the tree house.

Behind them, they heard the kitchen door bang.

Kathy realized she'd thought *he* would climb out via the roof, just as she and Timmy had. How stupid. Why should he? He'd merely run down the stairs and come out through the kitchen.

They might not make it after all.

Philip had disappeared, but, as they ran, Kathy had an urgent sense of his presence. And the horrible realization that *this* was why Philip's body had been found in the backyard.

He'd been trying to reach his tree house, too.

And that was why he was here tonight. Philip hadn't been saved, but his troubled little spirit was trying to save his good friend, Timothy.

They reached the oak tree at last. Kathy gave Timmy a quick boost. He climbed the ladder quickly, nimbly.

Kathy was a bit slower. She moaned under her breath. Why hadn't she worked harder at gymnastics this semester? Mitzi whining and struggling against her didn't help, either.

At last she reached the platform and was bending forward to pull up the rope ladder when she heard *him* reach the tree.

Then she felt a tremendous tug as he grabbed the ladder, wrenching it from her hands, and yanking it toward himself.

Kathy felt his weight—his deadly weight— as he began to ascend the ladder.

"Philip," he called. "Philip, are you there?"

"Yes, Daddy."

The voice came from the ground. Something silver glimmered beside the fishpond.

He turned, surprised. What was Philip doing down there? Why wasn't he in his tree house? Didn't he just see him go up the ladder?

All that running made his head ache. It was

getting worse, now. He could hear a terrible pounding, like a hammer on steel.

No, he mustn't let anything stop him. Not now. Not when he was so close to completing his mission.

His immortal sacrifice for all mankind.

And then, suddenly, the scarlet, pulsating thing that had lurked, undetected, in his skull all these years exploded.

A curtain of crimson blinded him and he fell.

And in that last micro-second before he died, he remembered . . . everything.

Oh God, he thought. Forgive me!

24

THANKSGIVING DAY, 1996

It's been more than a year now since Charles Winston tried to kill Timothy Colby. Even the small local paper has filed the story under "old news."

Kathy knows she will never forget what happened that night, but somehow the horror of it has lessened.

In the beginning, her main concern had been Timothy. Would he be marked forever? What would it do to him? And how would he feel about Philip? Would he remember him merely as one of his imaginary playmates or as what he really was—the ghost of a murdered child who had come back from the grave to save him?

Timothy has confused memories of Philip. And now, a year later, he thinks that maybe Philip might have been an imaginary playmate after all. He'd seen Philip's picture on the wall of *the tree house, he says, and somehow Philip had become real to him.*

Neither Kathy nor her parents argue with him about it. Mr. and Mrs. Colby aren't sure who or what Philip was.

Kathy knows, though. Just as she knows without a shadow of a doubt that the upper landing had been haunted by the spirits of Estelle Winston, her two older sons and their little black dog.

That feeling of listening on the landing—yes, it had been them. They'd been listening . . . listening . . . for the return of the man who'd killed them. Somehow they had known he would try to kill again.

There are no listening phantoms on the landing now. The grief and fear that bound the Winstons to earth has been resolved. They are free at last.

Timothy has grown up a great deal this past year. Knowing that he behaved bravely that night, helping to save not only his own life but probably that of his sister, has changed him. It has given him more confidence in himself, and a clearer sense of reality.

He rides a two-wheel bike now and has several friends in the neighborhood. He's into sports, too—Little League baseball and soccer.

But he doesn't go near the tree house anymore.

The tree house, now that it's not being used, has fallen into a premature decay. The boards have rotted and the little window is broken.

Timothy's sleeping bag and toys are still up

there. No one wants to go down to that part of the garden. The last storm broke off part of the old oak tree. Someday the Colbys will hire a crew to fill in the old stone fishpond and remove the tree with its weathered tree house. But not right now. Maybe later, when the events of that night aren't quite so clear in their minds.

But most of all, the Colby house is now a happy place, just as Mrs. Colby once predicted it would be. And on this Thanksgiving Day, a cheerful fire burns in the fireplace, and the smell of roasting turkey fills every nook and cranny of the house.

Matt will be coming over soon. He and Kathy are still going together. In fact, they are planning to attend the same college next year, one with a strong journalism department.

The doorbell rings. That must be Matt. Kathy smiles, smooths back her hair and runs to the door. Matt steps over the threshold and pauses for a moment to savor the warmth and sounds of the house.

No, not house. Home.

BABY-SITTER'S NIGHTMARES
Terror Beyond Your Wildest Dreams

ALONE IN THE DARK By Daniel Parker

A huge mansion on the beach, a fancy sportscar, a hot tub—and a kid who knows everything about Gretchen . . . including her deadly future!

A KILLER IN THE HOUSE By J. H. Carroll

Sue knows she shouldn't be sneaking around the Anderson's property after little Adam goes to bed. But baby-sitting can be so boring. Then Sue stumbles upon a strange envelope. An envelope with a mystery inside—a deadly mystery. Will Sue survive the night?

LIGHTS OUT By Bernard O'Keane

Something is coming for Moira. Something hungry. Something evil. Something that can't be stopped . . .

THE EVIL CHILD By M. C. Sumner

William is different from the other kids Toni's had to baby-sit for. He's smart— too smart. And he can build things—deadly things. And if Toni isn't careful, William may test his wicked inventions on her.

WHEN THE MOON IS IN THE
SEVENTH HOUSE...

BEWARE

#1 STAGE FRIGHT (LEO)
Lydia loves the spotlight, but the stage she is on is set for danger.

#2 DESPERATELY YOURS (VIRGO)
Someone at Fairview High will do anything for attention, and they may give Virginia a *killer* deadline.

#3 INTO THE LIGHT (LIBRA)
The line is blurry between Lydia's reality and her fantasy-world mural. What happens when her mural is slated for destruction?

#4 DEATH GRIP (SCORPIO)
Sabrina wants to avenge her boyfriend's death, which she knows was no accident—but revenge can be costly.